Pra

# Unapologetically Yours

"Warm, witty, and utterly addictive, Bitsy Yates's debut romance is everything I look for in a good read!"

—DEV FRIEDLANDER
A Purple Dragonfly Book winner, and author of *You See Me*

"This is a beautiful and astounding debut novel from Yates. You will not be able to forget the characters and their lives in a hurry. An immersive reading experience which will take you on a rollercoaster of emotions, heartbreak, and love. It will stay with you long after you finish the last page."

—GABRIELLE MCMASTER
Author of *Always Look Down*

"*Unapologetically, Yours* is a charming romance, set in a cozy, coastal town!"

—SOPHIA DESENSI
Editor at the Parliament House

"The setting of *Unapologetically, Yours* will draw you in to stay. With characters that are relatable, the story hits home, making Sayer and Isla easy to connect with."

—KEIRA FENZEL
Author

*Unapologetically, Yours*

by Bitsy Yates

ISBN 978-1-64663-529-0

Published by

◄ köehlerbooks™

3705 Shore Drive
Virginia Beach, VA 23455
800-435-4811
www.koehlerbooks.com

# Unapologetically, Yours

## Bitsy Yates

VIRGINIA BEACH
CAPE CHARLES

*To my dad, for always leaving me trails of encouragement from heaven. Thank you for always being my biggest fan, I love you.*

*From dream to dream and rhyme to rhyme I have ranged*

*In rambling talk with an image of air:*

*Vague memories, nothing but memories.*


**—WILLIAM BUTLER YEATS**

# Chapter 1

Marblehead Harbor, March 2020

As Sayer pulled his old, thirty-five-foot lobster boat into Beau's Port at Marblehead, he marveled at its unfaded beauty. It was just as he remembered. The saltwater spraying the rocks off the Massachusetts shore, the seagulls *singing* above him. His heart panged with regret at the memory of why he'd left, but he was grateful to be returning.

Sayer had to make sure to dock his boat carefully, knowing he would be judged if he messed it up.

"Welcome," a jolly voice called. A young boy held out his hand to catch the line. "How long will you be with us?"

"Not certain. A few nights at least," Sayer shouted, heading in at a steep angle to the pier. He turned sharply at the last moment to avoid hitting the bow.

"No problem, I'll get you all set," the dockhand said, grabbing the rope and tying his boat up.

"Thanks," Sayer smiled.

"First time here or returning?"

Sayer's gaze swept over the pier. "Returning, actually. I grew up here, but it's been a while."

"Welcome back, then!"

Sayer signed some paperwork and handed the young boy a ten-dollar bill. He knew that might be more than he should have given him, but remembered what it was like to be working your first job in high school.

"Thank you, sir," the boy grinned, shaking Sayer's hand with gusto.

"No problem, take care of her," he laughed. "I'll be back in a little bit."

As he turned the corner, Sayer passed a father and his young daughter on the dock with their fishing poles in the water. "That's it, now we wait," the man said, holding his daughter's reel with her on his lap.

"But daddy, when will the fishies come?" she asked in her raspy five-year-old voice.

"Soon, baby," he chuckled. "We have to be patient."

Sayer smiled at the image. This town had been a special place and still seemed to be. The blue sky was so vivid, it could have been fake. The sun peeked out of white clouds as a gentle breeze brushed the nape of his neck. *Such a great day for sailing,* he thought.

His stomach growled as he looked down at his old watch, noticing the small hand barely moving.

*Twelve-thirty.*

Sayer trudged up the wooden stairs to the old restaurant, Tina's. *The place was, and probably still is, a gem in Marblehead,* Sayer thought. With views of the harbor and sailboats, it was always nice to eat outside on the back deck. The perfect place to welcome him home.

This had been where he'd come with her. His sweet Isla.

She would always order chicken tenders with honey mustard from the kid's menu, which he found odd for a seafood restaurant. They would never question her though, even after noticing she was obviously an adult. She would watch the sailboats floating around, gawking at how slow some of them were moving.

*"I could never have that type of patience. I mean, you sometimes have to sit there and wait for the wind,"* he recalled her saying with a laugh. *"One time, my dad and I sat there for three hours waiting for the wind to move us."*

Sayer could sit there all day and just listen to her talk. The sun made her natural blonde highlights seem brighter, and her dimples would appear whenever she smiled or chewed her food. He noticed everything about her. He noticed that when she told a story, or recalled a memory, she told it with emphasis and excitement. He hoped she would never lose that spark, the embers glowing inside of her.

She would come alive with him, and he did not take that for granted.

"Hi, welcome," a waitress greeted with a warm smile as she wiped her hands on her apron. "Inside or outside?"

"Outside. The back deck would be perfect if there is room for one," he said.

"Yes, of course, I just cleared a spot in the corner. Is that okay?" She turned for him to follow.

"Sounds perfect."

Sayer slid on his Costas as he followed the young waitress. She dropped a menu on the table.

"Here you are. I'll be back in a few to get your order. Would you like to order a drink while you decide?" the waitress asked. Sayer quickly glanced at her name tag.

"Sure, Mya. I would love a sweet tea."

Mya looked at him strangely. "Sweet tea? I mean, I could bring you sugar packets to put inside of your iced tea?"

Sayer suddenly remembered where he was, *Massachusetts*. They didn't just make pitchers of sweet tea up here like he was used to them doing down in North Carolina.

"That'll be fine," he murmured.

She trotted off, and he glanced over the menu. It was completely the same, even the chicken tenders. His eye hesitated on them for longer than he'd intended. The waitress returned quickly to take his order, and she plucked the menu back.

He kept his gaze over the glossy water until the food came, when his eye was pulled upward. As the waitress pulled away, a lone figure shifted behind her, leaned on her elbows against a table at the other end of the outdoor patio.

Her long, blonde hair curled over her shoulder as she slowly turned the pages of her hefty book. Her lips curled into a smile, and her thumb played with the corners the way it always did.

His body went as still as a sail on a windless day. *Isla.*

The world stopped around him. Should he get up and walk toward her? Should he say hello? Would she be bothered by him? She'd never enjoyed being bothered while reading.

Last he heard, she was married, living with her husband in New York City, yet somehow, here she was, looking like a ghost from his memories.

Her eyes raised and caught his. "Sayer?"

"Mm, yeah, hey," he stumbled.

"Hi. It's Isla," she giggled. "How have you been? Care to join me?"

Her forwardness surprised him, but he didn't mind. Her soft, sweet spirit seemed to be untouched.

"Sure." He tried not to sound too eager. He grabbed his meal and brought it to her side. Nerves overwhelmed him.

She moved her sweating chardonnay glass closer and placed a stack of books to the side.

She smiled. Her dimples showed. Her beauty was as unfading as the town.

"How have you been? Still living here?" she asked, peeking through her lashes.

He straightened. She must not have been keeping tabs on him the same way he had been for her. "Actually, no, just visiting. See that old lobster boat over there?" he said, pointing it out. "I fixed it up in North Carolina, where I was living, and figured it would be nice to take it on a little adventure. It's still as beautiful here as it has always been," he said, admiring the view.

"That sounds like you," she gushed, taking a sip of her wine.

"Drinking this early?" he joked.

She sighed, slowly placing it back on the table. "Not early enough." Her face turned toward the sailboats. Sayer studied her rigid shoulders and tight lips, trying to read the story underneath. He could ask her about it, but it'd been so long, and it was no longer his place to look after her.

Silence surrounded them until she finally broke it.

"You know, sailing looks like a ton of fun, but—" she started.

"What? You don't have patience?" he finished.

"Yeah, exactly," she smiled. That smile could still turn his heart to knots.

Mya approached the table, eyeing the two of them together.

"Do you two need anything else?" she asked.

"I would love a Shock Top," Sayer said, smirking at Isla.

"Not a problem," Mya said, turning around.

"So, how long are you in town?" Sayer prodded.

"Not too sure. Kind of on a little vacation myself." Her voice dripped with the heaviness of a sorrow he couldn't identify, and she brought her eyes down to her lap.

He found himself speaking before he thought it through. "My plan is to be on my lobster boat for the time being. Not sure if you would be interested, but if you don't have any plans, I was just going to float around the harbor tonight. Wanna join me?" The breath hesitated in his chest, waiting for her reply.

Isla took a few moments to answer, taking another sip of her white wine. The corners of her lips pinched together in the way that they always did as she thought things through.

"Sure, why not?" she decided. "Like old times."

Sayers beer was placed in front of him. They took a drink at the same time. Her soft eyes matched the color of the sea. Smiling, he set his drink down.

"What?" she mumbled, grinning.

"You haven't really changed at all. Just a little older."

"Oh, thanks," Isla said, rolling her eyes.

"I didn't mean it in a bad way."

"Yeah, yeah," she whispered, then cleared her throat. "What time would you like me to meet you?"

"How about six? The water should be calm tonight and the sun will set not too long after that."

"All right, which boat is yours again?" Isla asked, looking over at the boats docked on the pier.

"That pale blue one, the last one near the end of the pier." He pointed.

"Got it. I'm going to go run some errands, but I'll see you later tonight." She finished her wine and picked up her keys and stack of books.

A dull ache nabbed him at watching her stand, but he pushed it aside. "See you later."

As she walked away, Sayer's gaze trailed her. Her small, curvy frame was still petite, her soft hair hit just past her shoulders, and her beige jacket crisply pressed. She always knew how to take care of herself, but never paused in front of mirrors to admire the masterpiece she so effortlessly created. He wondered—*hoped*—that same carefree girl he grew up with was still in there, somewhere.

Isla slipped into her car, resting her hands on the steering wheel, pausing for a moment.

"What just happened?" she whispered, fighting against the butterflies in her stomach. She glanced up, searching for one more look at the boy who'd once had her heart. Though her lips smiled, her mind spun.

Out of everyone in the world, why had *he* decided to come back to town? *Is he leaving something or someone behind in North*

*Carolina? That's a long way to travel just to see Marblehead again.*

Sayer still had that same quirky smirk he had in high school, the one he would use when he wanted to get out of trouble for something. She remembered one time in English class, he couldn't recall the author of *Wuthering Heights,* a book he had supposedly just finished reading. Their English teacher mocked him as he got up in front of everyone, spewing out quotes from the story to prove that he had read it. The teacher had put those exact quotes on the board for the discussion. The classroom erupted with laughter.

Watching him smile and trying to stick up for himself even though he was clearly lying, Isla knew at that moment she wanted to be like Sayer. She had yearned to learn that sense of playfulness that he so easily shared with others.

Without even trying, he'd challenged everything she believed in. How her parents told her that success came from college, or how a career is the path to happiness. Her life, once defined by rules and curfews, was so different from his.

He'd been the one to teach her how to live, regardless of what others thought of her.

Her fingers twisted the place where her wedding ring usually was. If only she'd not forgotten those lessons.

# Chapter 2

Marblehead Harbor, March 2020

*H*e rummaged around his boat, very aware that Isla would arrive at any moment. Sayer shoved the mess out of sight as best he could. On his way to the storage chest, right below the stern, he found a bottle of Merlot in the right-hand corner of the chest. A note was taped firmly in front of the label.

"That old man," Sayer whispered to himself, grinning ear to ear after reading the note. He tucked it inside his jean pocket.

Isla's slow steps echoed on the pier. The nerves grew inside Sayer as he soaked in the sight of her. The bright orange sky engulfed her frame. *What are we going to talk about? Will it be awkward between us?* Their last time together hadn't been the most pleasant.

"Hey, you made it." Sayer tried to keep his voice relaxed and natural.

"Hi!" Isla smiled. She stepped lightly down the pier. Her blue seersucker sun dress highlighted her tanned skin, the dress softly flowing in the wind.

"Thirsty?" Sayer asked. "I found this bottle of Merlot, figured you wouldn't mind sharing it with me."

"Is that because you caught me drinking with lunch today?" she laughed, running her fingers through her hair, fixing what the wind had blew around.

"Nah, not at all," he joked. "Just figured it might calm some nerves."

Sayer held out his hand to Isla as she approached the boat. "Be careful," he said, showing off that side grin she always said was adorable on him.

As their hands touched, Sayer couldn't stop the flood of memories. When they were high school juniors, he had invited her to Old Burial Hill on Halloween night. Knowing how much Isla loved anything spooky, he figured she would find this *date* romantic.

"Where are we going?" Isla had giggled. "It's so dark out!"

"Well yeah, that's kind of the point," he had smirked. "It is Halloween, after all."

"At least you brought a flashlight. Where are we going?" She had stared through the dark as fog settled over the trees.

"You'll find out soon enough," he had said as they walked down the winding road, red and yellow leaves rustling in their path.

"I think I know," Isla had whispered, holding Sayer's hand a little closer.

As they approached the old, steep stairs of the historical graveyard, they both looked up.

*Old Burial Hill.*

Isla and Sayer had not been foreign to the place. Often, when they were learning about the Revolutionary War in school, or the rich history of their town, the cemetery was mentioned. It was home to about 600 Revolutionary War soldiers, early settlers, sea captains, and fisherman and their wives and children. Some even dating back to the Mayflower.

"Let's go. What do you say?" Sayer had asked, holding up the flashlight and turning it on.

"Yes!" Isla's eyes had lit up.

"Here are the rules," Sayer stated, handing Isla her own flashlight. "Whoever finds the oldest dead person wins."

"What will I win?" she had asked while bouncing on her heels.

He had chuckled at her competitiveness. "Oh, so you're assuming you'll be the winner? *Go!*"

They had both darted up the steep stairs. The moon lit a path for them, and their breaths grew shallower.

"I came here in elementary school, and I do not remember these stairs being this steep," Isla had said, taking a break.

"Oh, come on, we're almost there," Sayer had urged. He laced his fingers in hers and pulled her the rest of the way.

When they reached to the top, the search had started. Both Isla and Sayer split up, shining their flashlights toward the tombstones.

Isla decided to go to the Orne Street side, where the tiny brick pathway led to a different section than Sayer, who had decided to go toward the top gazebo.

"Rebekah Bonfild, 1687," Isla had whispered, reading her epitaph. "Who did much good in her life." Isla couldn't help but wonder what these people were like when they were alive. *What good things did she do? Was she a teacher? Was she a fisherman's wife?* The epitaph did not specify.

Isla's eyes were drawn to a cluster of stones ahead on the brick pathway. Her flashlight had traced the name.

*In Memory of Mrs. Hannah Nowland*
*wife of Mr. Andrew Nowland*
*who died Janr. 6 1793*
*aged 21 years.*
*Also Hannah their daughter.*
*died Sept. 15th 1793 aged 12 Months*

*Twenty-one years old? That is so young,* Isla thought. She had wondered what they had died from. Illness? Her young daughter, only twelve months old, had died as well.

A short poem adorned the stone.

*All you that doth my grave pass by,*
*As you are now so once was I,*
*As I am now so you must be,*
*Prepare for death & follow me.*

She couldn't move from the spot. The leaves crunched as she sat down and read it again slowly, out loud to herself, the words making an imprint on her heart.

The message had hit hard.

Life was fragile, especially to those living back then. Had Hannah Nowland known she was going to die? Did she think that one day, people like Isla and Sayer would walk by her grave? Had she wanted her message to help someone? That even in death, she could help influence someone's thoughts to reflect on their own lives?

Perhaps it had been the graves speaking to Isla that night so long ago. Or perhaps it was the night seeping into her mind, making her question things. Isla thought then that she knew what she wanted in life, however, her wants had seemed divided.

One part of her wanted to graduate high school, go to college in Boston like her classmates, and live with Sayer in a tiny apartment above a bar downtown. Every night, they would joke how loud the restaurant was getting while sipping wine and eating spaghetti, because that was what they could afford.

It was a simple plan. And it was certain.

However, there was another part of her that had spoken louder. That part of her yearned to do something more than what everybody else was doing.

*What other options are there? Who will I meet at college? Should I limit myself to one person right now? What if there's someone else walking this earth that's meant for me? Someone to grow old with and who will support me?*

Those thoughts weighed upon her, and she couldn't shake them free.

She loved Sayer; that was undeniable. She couldn't help but wish they had met later in life, how much easier it would have been. Although they had another year together, she felt she could already see their end.

"Hey, who'd you find?" Sayer had called to her while walking in her direction.

"Oh, just some dead woman," she had muttered, not wanting to reveal its message. She didn't want Sayer to get any impression, as he tended to get philosophical.

"Well, I found this general from the Revolutionary War, I think I might have won," he had laughed, grabbing her hand and leading her to the direction of his grave.

That one gesture felt like a symbol of their future.

*Is that really what I want? To follow him forever?*

# Chapter 3

Marblehead, March 2020

"Iť's actually quite calm out there," Sayer said, pointing to the water. "Should be a nice night."

"Oh good," Isla smiled, "the sun is starting to set . . . look at that sky." Her face turned an amber hue.

Her beauty would always captivate Sayer. He found it difficult to turn away from. He popped the cork off the wine, filled the two glasses, and handed one to her.

"Thank you," she said.

They both sipped and looked at each other.

"Not bad, Sayer. I like this," she said, shifting the skirt of her sundress over her knees.

"Yeah, it's not too bad, huh?" he laughed, not wanting to tell her he had found it on the boat when he left Beaufort. He knew the old man, John, had put it there, wishing him luck.

Beaufort, March 2019

"Sir, are you selling this thing?" Sayer had asked, walking up to the old blue lobster boat in Beaufort.

"Trying to," he laughed. "I got to fix her up first, needs a new paint job and some electrical work done to her, but she's not that bad off."

"I could help," Sayer offered.

Sayer had been told sporadically throughout his childhood that his dad had a small fishing boat in Marblehead. He had never met his father, but of all the things his mom shared about him, from time to time, his love for fishing was a big one. Fishing was in his blood, and he knew it was something that would be a big part of his life as well.

"I wouldn't mind the company," the old man had agreed.

"Sayer, sir," he said, holding his hand out, slightly nervous.

"John, nice to meet you," he said, shaking Sayer's hand. "Just one thing."

"What's that?"

"When we're finished, you have to promise you are going to take this old lobster boat somewhere else. Somewhere you always wanted to be, got it?"

"Alright, deal."

Sayer started the lobster boat up, steering in the direction of Marblehead harbor. He figured he could drop the anchor once he and Isla were in the middle. Isla took a seat on the right side of the boat, holding her glass close to her lips. She placed her hand in the water, letting it glide across the top as the boat slowly moved forward. The warm water tickled her fingertips. Other boats were out, waiting for the sunset as well. It was always something to be marveled at. Something about it was calming to those that lived there, remembering the rich history that surrounded these New England waters.

"How's this?" Sayer asked, anchoring the boat in the center of the harbor.

"Great! I think other people had the same idea," Isla said, nodding in the direction of the sailboats clustered nearby.

Sayer took a seat across from Isla on his cooler, taking a big sip of his wine. Isla fidgeted with the edge of her dress, her eyes skirting over the boat and the water.

Sayer coughed. "What made you come back to Marblehead?"

Isla hesitated. She didn't want to reveal too much about her situation. He might not judge her, but being here was an escape. A place she always felt safe, secure.

"I just needed to get away for a bit."

"I understand that; life can get crazy." Sayer leaned back on one arm.

"What about you? Last I heard you were in North Carolina?"

"So, you have been keeping tabs on me?" he laughed, showing off that playful smile again.

Isla's cheeks grew rosy. Last year, she had attended their ten-year high school reunion downtown. While there, old friends were wondering where certain people were. Sayer was one of them. She had overheard someone saying that last they heard, Sayer was in North Carolina working on boats.

"I had just heard you were there," she took another sip of her wine, noticing her glass already becoming low.

"Yeah, I actually went down there after graduation. Felt I needed to get out of here, do something different than everybody else."

She knew that was a dig at her. The last time they had been together was the night before she left for the University of Vermont, just four hours north of Marblehead.

"How did you like Vermont?" he asked.

"It was . . .Vermont," Isla sighed, answering quickly. "Was there for four years and graduated."

She took another sip of wine. He'd been aware of how Isla's

mother had influenced her and how strict she was about Isla's future. Isla really didn't have a choice. She was going to the University of Vermont to study business so she could help her dad with their real estate business.

"Did you stop writing?" he prodded.

Isla had been the editor of their high school newspaper and then went on to become an advertisement manager for her college paper, *The Boson.*

"I did in college, but kind of stopped after that," she explained. "Didn't fit in the plan. I got rejected from a few literary magazines in New York. After that, it kind of killed it for me."

"That doesn't sound like you, giving up so easily," Sayer raised a brow.

They both quieted. As they finished their wine, Sayer lifted the bottle to Isla.

"Yes, please," she sighed, offering her glass to him. "So, what's your story? Why North Carolina?"

"Honestly? I just drove and stopped at the small town of Beaufort. I liked it so much, I decided to stay. I worked instead, saving up for a new adventure." He looked toward the water. "I thought coming back here first might help me figure out my next move, you know? Something about being back in these waters calms my thoughts, steering me in the direction I need to go."

Isla, after all this time, still wished she could have his courage. Not conforming to everyone's rules or expectations, doing exactly what he wanted when he wanted. It wasn't for everyone, that much she knew, but sometimes she wished she could know what it felt like to feel that free. She wished that for herself. Maybe one day she would achieve it.

"This place does do that, for sure. That's my reason for being back. You know, when life throws you curve balls, you tend to fall back on what's comfortable." She started feeling a little lightheaded, setting down her glass. She feared she would say too much if she kept talking.

Sayer studied her. How much of her pain did he see in her face? If he pushed, she'd break and tell him everything, but he refrained. He moved to lean against the taffrails and watch the moonbeams dance on the water, allowing her to keep her secrets.

It was a sign of respect she hadn't felt when they were last together all those years ago. She wondered how he felt about their last encounter, what he felt about her. *Is he still upset?* If so, he wasn't showing it—yet.

She messed with her finger again, it still feeling odd without her ring. Sayer's eye went to her finger, and she pulled it back.

"It's getting a little dark." Isla hugged her shoulders. "Chilly too."

Sayer reached for the plaid blanket laid over the cooler and tossed it to her. "Probably a good idea to head back."

She couldn't read his eyes as he steered the boat back in, only looking at her once.

Isla fixed on the wading of the waves, now dark as the night. Her chin tilted upward to the sky. "The stars are coming out," she breathed. It was a magnificence not often seen in New York City.

"Yeah, it's a pretty clear night despite the storm rolling in this weekend."

"There's a storm coming?" She shifted to Sayer, who inspected the horizon.

"A tropical storm, named Bertha. High winds and tons of rain."

"Great," Isla muttered. "Guess I'll be here longer than I thought."

# Chapter 4

Marblehead High, October 2007

"There is not going to be another discussion about it, Isla. You are going to the University of Vermont, that's that." Her mom set down the plate and moved to clean another one, brushing harder than necessary.

Isla rested her arms on the bar. "But Mom, how do you know that's what I want?"

"It's what *has* to happen. You can't do everything you want to do. It's not how life works." Her mouth set in a firm line, and Isla frowned.

"Dad doesn't even need my help. He has plenty of people working for him."

Her mom's sigh was long and drawn out. As she finished the plates, she moved to cut peppers, huffing with each stroke.

Patrice Wade was used to getting everything she wanted. Growing up in a well-to-do home, with both parents lawyers defending Bostonians, Isla's mother never worked hard for anything in her life. She met Isla's father, who was a family friend's son, right after college. Isla's father, Ben Wade, was the top real estate agent in Marblehead.

Selling homes faster than hotcakes, he knew how to charm the pants off anyone. Even if you weren't looking to sell your home, you seriously reconsidered it after having lunch with Ben.

Isla always wondered how her parents had met and fell in love. They never really talked about it. What she learned was that love was a business where one person works every day, even during holidays, to pay the bills and monitor the cash flow while the other spends money frivolously on expensive paintings nobody even looks at.

"Honey, just do as you're told, all right?" Patrice sighed, cutting the peppers with force.

Isla couldn't help but imagine herself as one of those peppers, her life being cut away from her with no say whatsoever.

"Whatever," she whispered, turning around and walking up the old creaky wooden stairs to her bedroom.

"*Whatever?* You don't say whatever to me," her mother roared, following her impertinent daughter up the stairs. Patrice was met with a slammed door.

Isla knew what she wanted, and being a real estate agent was not the future she imagined. As she sat on the window bench and overlooked the harbor, a tear slid down her cheek. Loss overwhelmed her. The loss of the life she hadn't yet even lived. Would she merely exist as this perfect robot of a person? Doing exactly what everyone expected her to do? Would she be successful?

Her parents had used that term so often, and yet Isla wondered if she even knew what it meant.

Isla watched as the waves slowly crashed against the rocks that surrounded their home, shielding it from the water, the white foam dancing between their peaks. The clouds were an angry dark gray, signaling an incoming storm. Trees bent under the growing wind.

She wished she could be those waves, drifting around wherever the current took her. Traveling to faraway places, carrying people on their own adventures, unaware of the storms ahead. Sure, storms would produce heavier swells, but as soon as it passed, it would calm again.

The ocean taught Isla so much more than any person ever could.

Harsher weather meant a shift in mindset, always returning to a calmer state. She prayed this storm in her life would pass, and that when the wind settled, she would be left with a life of her choosing.

In that moment, she made herself a promise. *I will never make the same mistakes as my parents.*

Her fingers itched for a pen to vent some of her anguish. Her mother knew exactly what buttons to push to anger her the most. Poetry calmed her mind, calmed her soul even. As she rummaged through her book bag to get her leather-bound journal, she came across a small note stashed away in her backpack. She slowly opened it, a smile washing across her face:

> *Everything about you is everything I need. I just hope that I can be everything you need. All I am giving you is me, but I am giving you all of me. I hope that is enough for the single most spectacular woman on Earth.*
>
> *I love you.*
> *I really, truly, love you.*
> *And that's all I can give.*
>
> *Love, Sayer*

If Sayer and Isla had a love language all their own, love letters would be it. Sayer was different. He spoke with his heart, letting his words move her. He knew how strained her and her mother's relationship was, and he often snuck notes into her backpack, hopefully to cheer her up when he couldn't be there. Isla read the note three times over. She knew their love would change her.

Isla reached for her cell phone and scrolled through to find the number of her best friend, Kelly.

"Hey, boo," Kelly said. "What's up?"

"My mom again, pushing her agenda on me. What are you up to?"

"Just painting," Kelly sighed. "It's not becoming what I want. Damn, your mom can't let it go, can she?"

"No, it's ridiculous."

"Does Sayer know that you are considering Vermont? What does he think?"

Isla curled her legs beneath her. "No, I haven't brought it up. There's no point. We still have all of senior year together, and I don't want that hanging over our heads like a storm cloud."

"True, no need to make decisions this early. I've got my heart set on South Carolina's Art Program, and I don't want to even think about how far away we're going to be from each other," Kelly muttered.

"Okay, now it's getting depressing." Next year would bring changes Isla didn't know if she was prepared for.

"My dad still isn't sure he wants me to move that far away from home," Kelly grumbled. "But he lights up as we talk about the art I can make there, so I suspect he's secretly excited for me."

"Good," Isla said, grateful her friend couldn't see her frown.

The conversations Kelly had with her parents about college were undoubtedly different than the dictate from Patrice to her daughter.

"You're going to do great things with the real estate business." Kelly's voice softened on the other end.

Isla played with the loose thread on the window seat. "My parents think so."

Kelly paused, her breaths rattling in the phone. Finally, she spoke again. "You're going to have an amazing life, Isla." Hope trickled through her voice, as if she could will it into existence, as if that's all it took, a few positive words to secure a happy future.

Isla could be so easily convinced. Her lips tightened, as her heart ached. She cleared her throat. "Listen, I need to get ready for dinner. I'll see you at school tomorrow?"

"Yup, see you then."

There was a hallow click as Isla stared at the phone in her hand.

"Dinner!" Patrice shouted, ringing the bell.

*That damn dinner bell. I wish she would just shove it up her—*

"Wash your hands, dear," Patrice insisted. "No need to get those germy hands all over my polished china."

Isla rested her head against the wall as she shouted back, "Why are we even using china anyway? Isn't that only for special occasions?"

Her mother's voice was chipper. "How do you know we don't have an announcement?"

Isla's heart sank. *Announcement? What could they possibly be announcing?* Her thoughts turned to Sayer, wishing he was there to comfort her.

Beaufort, May 2019

"Good morning, John, how are you doing today?" Sayer smiled.

The sun beat down on Sayer's neck as it reigned alone in the cloudless sky. That was always a regular thing in Beaufort, North Carolina. It wasn't Marblehead, but Sayer loved this small town with its close-knit community. It didn't take them long to welcome him in.

Beaufort had been his escape from Marblehead. But it just wasn't the same without Isla. He had escaped here to get away and clear his mind, in hopes of figuring out his own life, on his terms. He contemplated following Isla to Vermont, but what would that accomplish? He could feel her pulling away anyway and didn't want to be that anchor that weighed her down.

*People always say, if you're meant to be, you'll find your way back to each other.*

"Morning, son!" John placed a hand on the steering wheel of the lobster boat. "She's all right. Got her to start up this morning."

"Well, that's good. I bought the paint over the weekend to touch her up. Might look better with a new paint job," Sayer added.

"I think that'll help. You want to keep her blue?"

"I do, just a little lighter than the water, sir," Sayer insisted, holding out the paint cans for him to look at.

"I like it, looks almost identical to her original color," he smiled with a faraway look.

Sayer often reminded John of his own sons, handy with machinery and extremely smart, even if his smile sagged with a sadness he wouldn't disclose.

"Where's your family, sir? Around here?" Sayer inquired as he set the paint down.

"Well, I never married, but my two sons live in New York City, in Manhattan."

"That's a long way away," Sayer said, handing him a paint brush.

"Oh, you think I'm going to paint?" John laughed. "I don't think so," passing it back.

"That's probably a good idea," Sayer said, taking back the brush with a grin.

John settled back in his seat, watching the strokes as Sayer spread the paint over the wood. He filled the silence with tales of his younger days, and Sayer didn't care to tell him that he'd heard these ones already.

He'd share his own tales with John one day, when the ache for Isla wasn't so strong.

Marblehead, October 2007

At the dinner table, Isla had braced for the surprise announcement.

"Your father and I have been talking, and we had to move some things around for this to eventually happen," Patrice started.

Isla didn't want to move; she didn't want her mother to finish her sentence. She stared at her dinner plate, wondering what all those eating utensils were for.

"Are we moving?" Isla blurted.

"God, no," Patrice scowled. "Would you let me finish?"

"What your mother and I are trying to tell you is that we are expanding the family business, well, planted its seeds, so to speak," her father explained. "We are expanding the family to New York City. It's going to take a few years, but our thought is to set it all up and have it ready for you, Isla, after you graduate college."

"Isn't it splendid?" Patrice gushed, literally clapping her scrawny hands together, her gaudy rings clanging together.

Isla felt the crushing weight of despair settle on her back.

"Are you serious?" she muttered, not wanting to will it into the universe.

"So serious, honey," Patrice snapped. "We are setting you up for life. Now tell your father how excited you are," she smiled. "It's a done deal, your father just signed all the contracts this morning."

"Nobody thought to ask me?" Isla clenched her fists under the table.

"Obviously it's going to take a few years to develop, but we hope you will use that business degree to set your mark in the big city," her father chirped.

Anger knotted in Isla's chest, and she pushed back from the table. "That's it? It's all planned? Without asking me first?" She stood. "What if I don't want to study business?"

"Don't be difficult, Isla. Look at everything we have done for you," Patrice scolded, folding her napkin on her lap. "You'll be able to maintain this lifestyle for generations to come."

"*This* lifestyle?" Isla scowled.

Patrice's eyes carried fire. "This is serious, Isla. This is your future. Too many squander their years, and I won't let that happen to you. Being a writer is not realistic. Sayer is not realistic. His family is broken, and he doesn't have a stable home. I won't see you pulled into that."

"You aren't as smart as you think," Isla yelled, trying to keep tears at bay.

"That is no way to talk to your mother, Isla," her dad pointed.

"No, I'm done," Isla said, turning away and making her way to her room.

She knew where she was going to go—the Marblehead lookout across from the Old Burial Hill Cemetery. She grabbed her worn, leather-bound diary and went straight to the garage to grab her yellow beach cruiser. She placed her diary in the bike basket and angrily pushed the peddles.

*"Get back here!"* She could hear her mother yelling from inside.

Isla continued to ride while the hot tears in her eyes fell down her cheeks and the lump in her throat grew larger. Once she arrived at the lookout across from Burial Hill, she opened her diary, and with shaking hands, turned the page to a new one. She began to write with tears welling:

*One day, I will leave this town and never come back. I will be the person I want to be, not the person people expect me to be. As hard as I know it will be, I will leave this complacent state to pursue my own passions. I like to think, once I'm there, everything will turn out as it should have all along. All of these doubts will cease, and I will find my own happiness, on my own terms.*

The sun began to set as the trees around her quietly swayed. Isla could feel her heartbeat soften, the lump in her throat disappearing. Writing always did that; it always brought her back down to a place where she could finally think and say what she felt, without feeling judged. Sayer had also been that outlet. Whenever he was near, she felt like getting in his old Mercedes and driving wherever the road took them, wherever they wanted to go, leaving behind this town and everyone in it who tried to control them.

Isla felt a slight breeze, the winter wind creeping in. It would only be a few months until snow washed over this sailboat town. Isla loved the type of silence that came with the cold, the bitter truth it exuded. There was nothing like stepping outside into a snowy world and just listening. Everything would be glistening and quiet, animals burrowed inside their homes, fish gently swimming underwater, people inside by their billowy fires, surrounded by those they love. It was pure and real, something to look forward to at years' end.

As she turned the page in her notebook, a small and worn note slipped out. There it was, without fail:

*Every day that I am with you, I fall deeper and deeper in love with you. You still look at me the same way you did when we first met each other. You have no idea how much that means to me. You're the most stunning girl that I have ever seen.*

*Love, Sayer*

Tears that she felt had gone away returned with a vengeance. Her love for Sayer compounded each day, more than she could ever understand. She knew the life her parents had set up for her would not include him.

# Chapter 5

Marblehead, March 2020

"**W**ould you like to go to dinner tomorrow night? I'm staying at this Airbnb cottage with a view, and I have an easy recipe I want to try," Sayer smiled, trying not to show his nervousness.

Isla stood once they docked back at the pier, holding out her wine glass to him.

"You didn't like sleeping on your boat?" she teased.

"I just need more room," Sayer smiled.

"Sure, that sounds nice. Is six o'clock okay?" she laughed.

"Perfect. Here, let's switch phone numbers," he started.

"Mines the same," she smiled. "Unless you need it again."

Sayer remembered the night he deleted her number out of his phone. He was driving down to North Carolina, passing through Virginia. He knew that if he kept it, he would drunkenly text or call her, and he didn't want to give her that sort of satisfaction.

"I got a new phone, lost all my numbers," he sheepishly lied.

"Here, give me your phone, it's easier," she said, typing her number in his contacts. "Just text me the address."

"Okay, sounds good." He took his phone back.

"Tonight was really nice, Sayer. It reminded me of old times. I think I needed that more than you know," she said, getting off the boat and up onto the pier.

"Me too, brought back some memories for sure." He rubbed his hands together. "See you tomorrow?"

"Yes, tomorrow." She smiled, turning to leave.

Sayer watched the gentleness well up in her eyes as she spoke. Her smile slowly creeping up on her face, those dimples appearing. The pain of losing her so many years ago felt like a fresh wound. He tried to imagine her life now, and the life that could have been.

New York, March 2019

Walker took off his sports coat and hung it on the hook next to Isla's blazer. He placed his polished shoes neatly on the rack, then checked to be certain the door was locked. He dropped his keys on the marble kitchen counter next to Isla.

"My parents want to go to dinner with us this Saturday, and I already said we could. Seven o'clock okay?"

"This Saturday?" Isla looked up.

"Yeah, what else do we have going on?" He grabbed a glass and poured Scotch into it.

"I have dinner with Kelly. I haven't seen her in forever," Isla said, taking a sip of her red wine, watching its legs slowly run down the sides of the glass. "She's in the city for a work thing. I told you this."

"Honestly," he laughed, "I don't remember you telling me that at all."

"It's fine." She thumbed her glass. "I'm sure she'll be busy. I'll just reschedule."

He hardly looked her way. "Thanks, babe. My parents will be excited."

Isla got up and sat down on the sofa, next to the fire. She grabbed the cashmere throw blanket around her and held her glass up to her lips, the fire glaring against her face, warming her up.

"I'm going to take a shower, and then we can hang out. Did you make dinner?" Walker asked.

Isla rolled her eyes. "I ordered Chinese. It should be here any minute."

She shouldn't have caved so easily. They had just seen his parents, literally two weeks ago. *What do they have to talk about?* Nothing had really happened in two weeks that she knew of.

Isla turned off the TV and watched flames dance around the fireplace. The crackling of the fake, gas powered fire made her sad. She missed that smell of a real fire filling up the room; the slight hum of wood burning eased her mind, calmed her senses. If she could bottle up that smell of burning wood, she would have. Real fireplaces were almost obsolete in New York, especially in pricey apartment complexes, such as theirs, off Central Park.

"Is that the door, babe?" Ben shouted from the loft above her.

"Oh, yeah, I'll get it," she said, placing her wine glass on the wooden coffee table.

Isla tipped the delivery guy and closed the door. "Smells delicious," Walker said, helping her with the bulky bag of food.

"It does; god, I love Chinese food," she smiled, opening the bag and placing the cartons of food on the counter. "Chopsticks?" she offered Walker.

"Thanks," he said, grabbing them from her. "I am so hungry; I missed lunch today."

"Meetings?" She dug her chopsticks into her lo mein noodles.

"Yeah, another proposal meeting." Walker shrugged. "I might be late coming home this week, FYI."

"Oh, okay," Isla muttered, pretending to not let it affect her.

Walker and Isla met after college graduation, her from the University of Vermont, him from Stanford. He was athletically built, six-two, brown eyes; she was five-ten, thin but toned.

Their parents grew very close in their absence. Walker's father, Robert Williams, owned a Brewery in Marblehead, which blew up as soon as it opened. Walker helped his dad with the marketing side of things. With views of the harbor, the Brewery grew to be a very popular place for people to relax in their Adirondack chairs, sipping cold craft brews as they watched the tide roll in. Walker's father was proud of his business and what he had created, as he should have been. Often, their conversations were about some new brew he had made and how popular it was becoming. It had been Walker's mother's idea to open the venue up for weddings, which proved lucrative.

Walker and Isla were married there, just a few short months ago. It was a quick engagement, only four months. Both families were so excited and planning just seemed to take off. It was a beautiful ceremony attended by three hundred guests. Isla felt that was a little overkill, but the families didn't relent.

"Are you alright?" Walker nudged her. "You seem out of it tonight."

"Oh sorry, just thinking about work," she lied.

"Oh yeah, how's that new building coming? Any bites yet?"

Isla twirled her noodles around her chopsticks.

"Kind of, just trying to finish a few things before we show it," she explained. "New light fixtures are being replaced, and they were kind of expensive, but I think they make a statement. Trying to hold off until those are in. I also got a call from our sub-contractor today that they are backordered and not available for a few more weeks," she sighed.

"Oh, yikes," he said, a mouthful of egg roll rolling around in his mouth. "Does your dad have any contacts you could call?"

Ever since Isla took over her dad's real estate company in New York City, she had hit roadblock after roadblock, disaster after disaster. Her clients were uppity and demanding, not something she had been used to in Marblehead.

*It's fine,* she'd remind herself. *It's not for forever.*

Someday, she'd tell her parents she was leaving New York City, as soon as she figured out her next plan. And found the courage to do so.

"Probably, but I have to figure it out on my own," she said, taking a sip of her pinot noir.

"Yeah," Walker scoffed. "Okay."

Later that evening, they made love. It was quicker than she anticipated, and afterwards, Walker fell asleep on his side of the bed. Isla lay there, a single tear rolling down her cheek. She wiped it away and turned her back to him, looking out her window at the city down below. She loved Walker, but something was missing. *Passion.* She had thought it was there, but after being married a few months, she quickly felt it fizzle away.

Her heart ached with resentment. Her thoughts turned to Sayer.

Marblehead, March 2020

Sayer wanted to impress his old heartthrob, to show himself worthy. And the one thing he knew he could do was appear to have a clean place, even though he was just renting for the time being. When they were younger, she always marveled at how clean his room was, and his '85 Mercedes. Sayer liked to keep things neat and tidy, but not more than his mother, who was always reminding him to do so.

Luckily, it paid off.

Sayer looked down at his old, whiskey barreled watch, and noticed he had forty-five minutes until her arrival. He turned the hot water on and slid his shirt over his tanned, broad shoulders. Steam quickly started to cover the vanity mirror, much like his nerves taking over his thoughts.

Afterwards, he pulled on a buttoned blue and white plaid shirt with some khaki shorts and, of course, his Rainbow flip flops. He strategically sprayed his cologne on both sides of his neck, the same cologne he's always wore, and brushed his dirty blonde hair off to the side. He hoped Isla might remember it's soft scent when he went in for a hug.

*Five forty-five.*

*All right, time for some music.*

Sayer thumbed through the vinyls stacked beside the record player until one stood out. He slipped the record out of its casing and gently placed it on the platter, lowering the cartridge until he heard the scratchy beginnings of an old song.

*Perfect,* he smiled.

*Five-fifty.*

Knock, knock.

*Shit,* he thought, *running his fingers through his damp hair one more time.*

"Hi." Isla smiled sweetly as Sayer opened the door.

"Hey, come on in." He stepped back for her to enter.

"Those are beautiful," she said, delicately touching the white gardenias on the center of the table.

"Oh yeah, thanks, I picked those up earlier," he mentioned, trying to sound coy.

"Where should I put my jacket?" she asked, taking off her light coat.

"Here, I'll take it." He held out his hand and hung it on the coat rack behind the door.

"Thanks," she said.

As she turned around, soaking in the Jack Johnson playing in the background.

It took her right back to when they were kids, driving down the road after school.

"Wine?" Sayer asked, holding out a glass to her.

"That would be great." She wrapped her fingers around it. "What's on the menu for tonight? It smells delicious."

"Well, I hope you still like seafood." he smiled. "But there are a few more minutes on this orange ginger salmon I've got going," he said, opening the oven to check on it.

"That does sound good. You know I'm always up for salmon."

Sayer stirred the steamed vegetables and steamed potatoes as Isla slipped off her white sandals near the door and paced the small New England, Airbnb beach cottage. Outside the white-pained window was the tall lighthouse overlooking the rocky shores of the harbor.

Isla smiled. *That's why Sayer picked this place.*

"This is lovely." She ran her hand along the white shiplap covering the walls.

"Yeah, I think the owners mentioned the shiplap is all original to the house, just restored," he said from the kitchen.

"It's beautiful. I love how cozy it is." She touched the mismatched throw blankets near the big bay windows.

"I think it is too, plus that view." Sayer pointed to the sunset, then wiped his brow.

Isla plopped down on the sectional like she had been living there for years. She curled her leg under the other and placed her right arm on the back of the couch, her body positioned toward the harbor, her left hand holding her wine glass. As she took another sip of the citrusy chilled wine, she felt a calmness wash over her, something that had been missing the entire months Sayer had been away in Beaufort. She felt it was okay to breathe again, to be herself. Sailboats were slowly moving effortlessly across the water, the wind gliding them on like butter, many heading south ahead of the winter. The harbor looked like glass, shiny and untouched.

Sayer brought everything to the table. "Ready to eat?"

"Yes, it looks great," she said, standing up and walking toward the table. Sayer's eye traced her as she placed the linen napkin over her lap.

"We don't need to be that formal," Sayer joked.

"Well, if I get anything on these jeans, I'll be pissed," she laughed.

Sayer mocked her by placing his own napkin on his lap. "Still a clumsy eater then?" She shot him a look.

They both handed each other the bowls of food, clinking the serving spoons against the porcelain.

"I hope it tastes okay," Sayer said. "If not, we can always go grab pizza down the road."

Isla took a bite, her blue eyes widening, "No, this is good!"

"Really? Thank God," he sighed. "Catching fish is always super easy for me, but cooking it is a different story. I always seem to dry it out."

She took another bite. "You nailed it this time."

"So," Sayer said as his fork scraped against his plate. "Still talk to Kelly?"

Isla's stomach turned. "A little. We sort of had a falling out. She doesn't like my husband very much."

It slipped and her eyes darted toward her plate.

"Husband?" Sayer asked, lowering his glass, clinking his knife accidentally. He looked to her empty finger.

"Um yeah, kind of," she mumbled, trying to figure out how to explain this.

"So, you *kind of* have a husband?" His brow furrowed.

Isla shifted in her seat. "It's a long story. We're separated; he just doesn't know it yet."

"How does he not know?" Sayer leaned forward in his seat.

"I sort of left . . . and came here . . . without formally telling him myself." She glared at her shaking hands.

"Hmm," Sayer said, patting his napkin across his lips. "Interesting."

She peeked up at him. "Why do you say that?"

"You're very, well, you used to be, so structured," he said. He looked at her in a funny way, as if he was trying to read her mind. Isla ducked her head.

"Well, I did leave a letter."

Sayer laughed, drawing a smile from Isla.

It was so true; she craved structure when she was younger, getting into college, diving into a good, albeit arranged, profession. One part of her needed that, but the other part that seemed to be rattling in its cage more frequently, wanted so desperately to be set free. The part of her that also longed for adventure and the unknown. The part suppressed for fear of failure. But how do you fail at adventure? She often wondered, but now realized, you fail only when you never feed that specific desire. She learned, after many years, that once you stop feeding something, it starts to find food elsewhere, in your dreams, even. Taking over your subconscious and haunting your thoughts, causing you to doubt your choices.

She knew she needed a change, and Marblehead was the first place she could think of to quiet those thoughts.

New York, November 2019

On his way home from the airport, Walker picked up his iPhone to call Isla, knowing how much she probably missed him.

"Hey, I'm back in town, love. Want to grab a bite to eat?" Walker asked, weaving in and out of the traffic down Fifth Avenue.

"Sure, let me get changed and I'll be down in a bit. How far out are you?" Isla asked, checking in the mirror to see that the bun on top of her head was still intact.

"Just a few minutes."

"Okay, sounds—" the phone clicked as he hung up. "Good," she sighed.

Walker had been away for two weeks on business in Charlottesville. He and his dad were trying to expand their business to Virginia, hoping to find a space to takeover. Their New York Brewery, *Time Hop*, had opened about a month ago and was doing quite well. Walker was in charge of that one, taking on full responsibility. He was used to working late hours and chatting with customers, and he thrived in that environment. Plus, drinking beer was a perk as well.

Isla grabbed her ivory winter pea coat and her cognac leather purse and headed to the elevator. It had been a full two weeks since they had seen each other. She missed him, but now she'd greatly miss the quietness of the apartment and the ability to binge whatever show she wanted without Walker complaining.

"Hi babe," she said, sliding into the front seat of his blacked-out Ford Explorer.

He rested a hand behind her neck. "You look nice."

Isla winced. Even though it had been two weeks, the bruise he had left before he left was still fresh.

She covered up her pain with a smile. "Thanks," she said, crossing over to click her seat belt in. "Where do you want to go?"

"How about Hugo's?" he asked. "I could go for their steak salad."

"Sure, sounds fine," Isla turned her head to watch out the window as all the people passed by.

"Just fine?" Walter questioned. His tone and expression turned angry, his brows knitted, and mouth set in a line.

Isla didn't want to rattle things. "It's perfect," she corrected herself, smiling back at him.

He nodded, and she turned back to the window.

New York charmed her in a way she hadn't expected. It was so much different than Marblehead, and maybe that's what she found appealing. Everyone that lived there had somewhere to be, places to go. They all looked like they were on a mission, so important.

The gray clouds took over the sky, the bitterness of winter setting in. The heated seat started to kiss her skin, feeling the warmth beneath her jeans.

"Looks like it might snow," Isla said, breaking the silence. "I love New York in the winter."

"You might be the only one," Walker chuckled, turning into the restaurants valet stand. "Ready?"

As soon as they got out, Walker slipped his hand into hers to lead her into the restaurant. He moved his hand to the small of her back as he held the door open for her and gave her another smile.

"You're gorgeous," he whispered, his cheek gently brushing hers. "I'm a lucky man."

It was moments like this that she knew, deep down, Walker was a gentleman.

If only he could learn to control his temper.

The next day, Isla was at her desk in her office when he stormed in, and her adrenaline shot right through her veins.

"We need to talk." Walker's arms were crossed and his face solemn. He paid no regard to any looking his way.

"Can we talk about this later? I'm kind of busy," Isla mumbled, shifting her eyes over the nearby agents. They brought their heads back to their desks.

"Not really." He walked down the hall to the conference room. He peeked back once to be sure she followed.

Isla rolled her head back to sigh. She got up, tucking her skirt as she stood, and rolled her chair under her desk.

Everything was on Walker's time. If it wasn't in his plan, it rarely happened.

"Have you seen this yet?" Walker said, holding up his phone.

Isla shut the door behind her. "Seen what?"

"Are you serious?" He passed her the phone, and his voice dropped to a whisper. "Isla, your dad passed away."

Her breath froze in her body and the floor swayed beneath her feet. Her heart swelled up, closing in on her throat.

Walker shifted on his feet. His forehead creased. "What is this going to do to our business?"

"He what?" Isla stammered. Her hands shook as she stared at the phone. "How is this possible? I just saw him at Thanksgiving," Isla said.

"I know, but Isla, the business," he pushed, raising his voice.

Her eyes trailed up to him. "The business?" Words weren't making sense.

He sighed, taking back the phone and holding her hands in his. "Our business. This real estate business. We have to be sure it'll be fine without him."

She shook her head. "No, no, he was always so active," she said. She winced as she realized she was already using the word *was*.

"Honey, we need to be certain our financial future is secure."

Her lips parted. *Financial future.*

Was it no longer customary to apologize when your wife loses a loved one? Where was the sorrow for how her heart must be breaking? Where was the reassurance that he'd be with her through the pain?

"I don't know what to say," he said, throwing his hands up in the air.

It took her a moment to speak.

"You never know what to say." Her angry eyes filling with tears, and she took a step away from him. "I'm walking home alone. I need to be by myself right now."

She felt a pinch at her arm, his fingers tightly wrapping around her forearm, her heart at a standstill.

"Stop." She tugged her arm, looking up at him, half afraid of how he'll respond to her standing up for herself.

"Really? You think you can tell me to stop?" His breathing was fast and his eyes dark. His grip tightened.

"Not here," she bit back a cry. "This is my office."

"*Our* office," he corrected her. He released his grip, but his words stung just as hard. "You're nothing without me."

Isla fled the room.

Cold wind nipped her face as she stumbled to the streets where horns honked, and angry New Yorkers' voices bit the air. She wrapped her arms tightly around herself and buried her chin into her scarf, wishing she could hide from the world.

The world had grown darker since this morning. Now it was bitter and hallow.

She'd taken over the business so her dad could retire. Without him, there was nothing tethering her here.

Her phone vibrated and she cursed, preparing herself for whatever cruel words Walker had sent.

It was her mother's name that appeared instead.

Isla pressed the phone to hear over the busy streets. "Mom, how are you?"

Her mother was frantic on the other end. "Why haven't you been picking up? I've been trying to call you all afternoon."

"I'm so sorry. I was with clients in a closing. My phone has been in my bag."

"Isla, your father died." Patrice said. "Heart attack. I'm going to need you to come back to Marblehead, as quickly as possible." Isla searched for the pain in her mother's tone, but if her mother wept, it didn't show.

"Of course."

"How fast can you be here?" she asked, hastily.

"Well, let me look at the flights and I'll text you," she said. She'd said the same thing many times over in business transactions.

Her mother ended the call without another word.

That was the second person to inform her of her father's passing without asking if she was okay. Isla took a deep breath as she lowered herself to a park bench. As long as she focused on something else, she could keep the tears at bay, at least until she got home.

She went onto Southwest's website and booked the earliest flight out. She texted her mom to let her know. Her mother insisted she would send a car to pick her up at Logan in Boston. Her weary gaze lifted to her apartment building as emotions swirled within her.

She had a big decision to make.

Marblehead, March 2020

"More wine?" Sayer offered.

"Of course, is that even a question?" Isla laughed as Sayer filled her glass with a chilled sauvignon blanc. Their washed dishes lay in the sink behind them as the moon shed a pale light through the window.

"Do you want to sit in the covered sunroom? I can put a fire on," Sayer suggested.

Isla had no desire to leave. "Sure."

They grabbed their drinks and headed for the back door, Sayer opening it and letting her go out first. Isla's bare feet touched the warm floor and brushed the overhanging leaves of plants in pots around them.

"You water all these?"

"Hah!" Sayer laughed, "they actually have a timed irrigation system in those flower beds, so I don't have to water them at all."

"Oh, that's clever." She crossed to the window to stare over the harbor as Sayer ignited the fire. Soon, the warmth filled the room.

Or perhaps that was due to how close he was to her.

"I'm glad you decided to come back to Marblehead," Sayer confessed.

"Me too," she smiled, curling her hair around her ear, exposing her neck. "Just wish it would have been under better terms."

"I'm sorry," he whispered. His hand flickered like it might reach for hers, but it stilled.

She turned and leaned against the wall so her body faced his. "Did you know my parents don't live here anymore?"

"What? Your dad basically owned this town," Sayer joked.

Isla's gaze dropped to her drink. "They retired two years ago to Williamsburg, Virginia, but decided to keep our home here for the summers." She swallowed the lump in her throat. "Dad just passed, actually. That's why I'm here. My job, according to my mom, is to sell our family home, cut ties with this town."

Sayer's eyes dropped, "I'm so sorry, Isla."

There it was, the normal reaction she'd expected from someone after hearing of a death. It comforted her more than she could say to hear him say those words. His hand settled on her arm and stroked for a moment before it fell back at his side.

She gave him a slight smile. "I'm basically finished putting the house on the market, now just waiting for a buyer. But I won't be returning to New York."

"Really?" Sayer asked.

"Yeah. Nothing good for me is there anymore." She turned back to face the harbor.

"So, how'd you make it to New York anyway? I don't remember that being in your plan," he gently asked.

"Before retiring, and while I was still in college, my dad expanded his real estate group to New York, basically built it up while I was in college. Once I graduated, I took over so he could retire. It's worked out, but it's a lot of work," Isla explained.

"I see," he mumbled. "Is that what you want to do?"

"I mean, it brings in a lot of money, but I don't sleep, often working all hours of the day, and forget about weekends."

"But is that what you want to do?" he asked, again.

Isla paused, now understanding the depth of his question.

"No, not at all," she sighed, feeling a weight lift off her shoulders.

"Then why put yourself through that?"

"That's the reason I'm here. I'm trying to figure me out, to figure out what I truly want. You might remember my parents; I didn't have a choice."

Sayer stopped probing and stared over the water. He didn't say anything for a long time.

Isla sighed. "It's so hard, you know. On one hand, I know what's best for me, and on the other, I'm afraid of failing on my own," she explained.

"I get it." Sayer nodded. "Your parents, mainly your mother, were never the easiest."

"Right?" she said, grateful for someone who understood.

"I think you're doing the right thing now by taking time for yourself."

"I already feel clearer." She took a deep breath. "Like I can finally breathe again."

Sayer smiled. This was what he'd told her to do, all those years ago. To pursue her own dreams with all her might. It'd taken her far too long to listen to him.

His hand grazed hers.

They both stood there for a moment, soaking it in. The sun was setting, creating a beautiful hue of red and gold, consuming the ocean beneath it. She didn't move her hand away, staying completely still. She wished she could freeze this moment, everything except the goosebumps that were slowly creeping up her arm. He was still as electrifying as ever; that, she could not deny.

# Chapter 6

Beaufort, July 2019

"You all right, Sayer?" John asked, pausing from his stories.

"What?" Sayer asked, dipping his paint brush in the warm blue paint bucket, continuing to brush the lobster boat.

"You seem quiet today."

"Oh, I'm fine." Sayer brought his brush back to the boat.

"Don't piss on my leg and tell me it's rainin'!" John scoffed.

"All right, fine," Sayer admitted, smiling. The old man had a weird expression for everything.

"It's a girl, isn't it?" John laughed before Sayer could say anything.

He looked over his shoulder. "How'd you know?"

"Does a bear shit in the woods?"

Sayer smirked. "It's complicated," he said.

"It always is with the right ones," John said. "How about you come over tonight for dinner? I have plenty of food, wouldn't mind the company."

"I have no plans, so that works for me. Thanks," Sayer smiled.

"And you can tell me just how complicated she really is," John offered.

Later that night, Sayer pulled up to his house, his old Ford truck rattling as he pulled the keys out of the ignition. He opened the door as John came out to meet him.

"Hey, you made it." John smiled, patted him on the back.

"Told you I would."

"Wanna beer?" John offered, handing him a Busch can.

Sayer cracked it open as they walked up the creaky stairs to his front door.

The homiest smell greeted them, something sweet and warm. John walked through to the kitchen, opening up a beer himself.

"Who is this?" Sayer grinned, bending to pet the white fluffy dog. He looked back to John. "Wouldn't peg you for a poodle guy."

"You watch it." John laughed. "This is the best dog I'll ever own."

"I bet."

"Well, come on in. Want to watch the end of the game with me while dinner finishes up?"

"Sounds good," Sayer said, plopping himself on the worn padded couch. "Who's playing?"

John's mouth dropped open. "You don't follow football?" He waved a hand over the TV. "Even the president's there."

Sayer shrugged. "Not too much . . . not really my thing."

"I wouldn't go around telling people that," John joked, shaking his head. "Army versus Navy. Obviously, I want Navy to win." He nodded to his old uniform, now framed on the wall.

"Got it, that makes sense."

John sat in his recliner beer to his lips. "So how about telling me about that girl?" he chuckled. Sayer started from the beginning, talking about his high school years.

Marblehead High, October 2007

"Hey, you," Sayer smiled, slipping into the chair next to Isla. "Good morning."

"You're supposed to be quiet." She nudged him. "This is the library."

"Eh, Mrs. Jones loves me," he said, waving in her direction toward the checkout desk. "What are you studying?"

"Trying to study," she corrected him.

"Why?" He plopped his backpack on the table, opening its tattered zippers.

"Ummm, for our quiz this morning." She showed him her flash cards. "Remember?"

"Well, I forgot." He scooted his chair in. "Let me quiz you."

Sayer gently plucked her cards from her hands. "All right, first question. Are two atoms of the same element identical?"

Isla stared blankly at Sayer.

"All right, let's just try another one," he said, sifting through the cards. "Why do atoms contain the same number of electrons and protons?"

Silence.

He tossed her back the cards that she so desperately needed. "I mean, did you study them?"

"Apparently not those exact ones." She straightened the cards with a frown.

Sayer grinned as she chewed on the end of her hair and sifted through the notes. She tried so hard—mostly in vain— to understand chemistry. The morning bell rang, alerting them to head to their first class.

"Let's get this over with," he said, holding Isla's hand. She chewed on her lip.

They walked together down the hall, each step leading Isla closer to her doom. As they stepped in, their teacher, Mr. Carey, looked up, and their hands slipped away from each other. Sayer took his seat up front, Isla a few chairs behind in the next row.

"Everything off your desks except a pencil and your calculators," Mr. Carey instructed, his dark hair and beady eyes watching that everyone was doing what he said.

Sayer looked back at Isla who was rolling her pencil in her hand. She always did that when she was nervous. She looked up and he gave her a smile and a small wink.

Isla grabbed the quiz that was passed down to her and she glanced at the first question:

*Why do atoms contain the same number of electrons and protons?*

She smiled, looking up at Sayer who let out a small laugh.

Beaufort, July 2019

"She's not like anyone I've ever met. I'm not sure if it's just because she's not mine anymore, but I miss her every day," Sayer explained, adjusting his seat in the puffy sectional, feeling comfortable talking with John. He had this personality that made you feel exciting.

"Do you ever talk to her anymore?" John asked.

"No. We sort of cut ties the night she left for college. Her family made it very clear we wouldn't be together. After that, I worked at the pier at Beau's Point back in Marblehead, saved some money, and drove here. I just drove and didn't really stop until I got here. I heard the fishing's good, something I grew up doing."

"I see, so you ran from it all?" he raised a brow.

Sayer pondered that for a few moments and took a sip of his beer, "Well, I guess I did."

"Nothing worth having comes easy, son. Trust me, if she is worth something to you, sometimes you have to fight for it. It might not be on your own timeline, but love always finds its way back if its right. It sounds cliché, but it's true." He smiled.

"I'll keep that in mind," Sayer said, finishing his beer.

# Chapter 7

Marblehead, March 2020

I sla took a sip of her white wine, feeling the citrus burst onto her tongue.

"Want to go sit by the water?" Sayer asked, walking toward the white Adirondack chairs that sat at the top of the grassy hill while the water slapped against the rocks below.

"Isn't it freezing?" Isla asked.

"Not with a bonfire." Sayer grinned. He grabbed a few pieces of wood and a lighter. They silently walked next to each other, tension rising.

"How's your mom?" Isla asked, sitting down.

"Oh, she's good, still living on Washington Street," he smiled, lighting the fire. "Still painting."

Her paintings were exquisite. When they were kids, she would be in the sunroom, paint everywhere, drawing on both large and small canvases, with folk music playing. She loved to paint the ocean, but more importantly, people and families there, enjoying the sun and water.

"I always loved her," Isla gushed. "Almost as much as you," she laughed, feeling her wine whisk her caution up into the air.

"I know," he laughed, putting his glass down onto the rough arm of the chair. "I think she might have loved you more than me."

"Yeah, yeah," she smiled.

"You know she loved your writing, especially your poetry."

Isla remembered. "She helped me figure out my senior project, a series of poems. She was painting while I was writing. Where were you?" she laughed.

"No idea. Not sure it even mattered."

They both sat in silence, smiling. Back then, Isla lived at their house. There were few rules there, just love, honesty, and lots of burning candles. It was only her and Sayer. His father wasn't in the picture and Sayer never spoke about him, but Isla always wondered if he ever wanted to.

His mother, Gaila, had the purest soul. She always wore a smile on her face and her arms were wide open. Whenever they made dinners in her kitchen or homemade thumbprint cookies near Christmas, she was always around, her happiness poured over them like icing on a cake. She lit candles everywhere, the smell of kitchen spice filling up the home. It felt so welcoming to Isla. During the winter, there were always crackles from the roaring fireplace waiting for an audience.

When Isla fought with her own parents, she felt peace after talking with Gaila, often sharing a pint of Cherry Garcia ice cream. She had a unique perspective of the world, so calm and optimistic. When she listened to you, you felt heard and cared for.

New York, January 2019

When Isla walked in, she didn't see Walker.

"Walker? You here?" she shouted, walking up to their bedroom in the loft of their apartment.

Not hearing a sound, she opened their closet door and grabbed her suitcase. She went through her drawers and packed the essentials: her two cardigans, her favorite pair of denim jeans, a few basic tee's and her khaki Ugg boots. She went into the bathroom and grabbed her shampoo, conditioner, hairbrush, and makeup bag. Everything else she could buy if she really needed it.

She flew down the stairs with her bag in hand and searched for paper. On the island, she wrote a letter:

*Dear Walker,*

*With my dad's passing, my life has suddenly turned upside down. I'm not sure if I'll ever be back to this apartment, or this city. You can have everything. You have taken every ounce of me away from myself; it's time I find what I need, what my soul needs. Deep down, you could have never made me happy.*
*We both know we weren't meant for each other.*

*Isla*

With a single tear, she picked up her bag, opened the door, and let it close behind her. Her tears were not of sadness, but of relief. As she stepped out onto the cold, snow filled street, she raised her arm to hail a cab, the light snow encapsulating the trees of central park, the glow of the streetlamps illuminating the slick path beneath them.

She would miss the city, but more importantly, she was going to finally fulfill the promise she had made herself so long ago.

Her life had truly begun, on her own terms.

She nuzzled into her window seat on the flight while an older gentleman took his seat next to her.

"Good night for a flight," he said, folding up the tray in front of him.

"I hate flying, to tell you the truth." She released her tight grip on her bag to hold out her hand. "I'm Isla, by the way."

"John." His steady grip shook her hand. "So where is a young girl like you off to?"

"Home, actually," she sighed. It wouldn't feel like home without her dad there. She sucked in a deep breath to keep tears away. "It should be a quick flight for me."

"Where's home?" He tucked his bag under the seat and folded his coat over his lap.

"Marblehead, Massachusetts, right next to Salem. About thirty minutes from Boston."

His eyes lit up. "Oh yes, I know Salem well. So much rich history."

"It has plenty of that," she said with a sad smile. For her, it held memories of people now gone.

The plane moved backward off the gate, and Isla clenched the arm of her seat. Her eyes were glued to the window. The flight attendants were busy telling other passengers to lock up their tray tables and to put their phones away.

"You know, I've flown a lot," John whispered, gently leaning toward her. He eyed her white knuckles. The lights above them dimmed and the cabin grew quiet as the plane accelerated toward the tarmac.

"Yes, I love it. Nothing safer, that is if the pilot knows what he's doing."

Isla's head snapped up. "What?"

John chuckled. "You'll be fine. The plane basically drives itself. It's all computers now."

Isla's grip loosened. "I hope so. Enough things have gone wrong today." She rubbed her thumb over her finger where the indent of the ring could still be seen. Her finger was empty as was the place in her heart her father once filled.

John offered his hand. "You'll be fine," he nodded. "I have a good feeling about you."

"Thank you," she said, holding his warm hand, and a small smile brushed across her face.

Marblehead, March 2020

Amber colors brushed across the sky as the sun dipped below the town's horizon. The wind picked up as the waves rolled in. Sayer handed her a green plaid quilt to place around her shoulders. Sitting in their chairs overlooking the water, Isla felt something familiar—a sense of belonging. She turned her head to look at Sayer as he took a sip of wine. His face was cleanly shaven, so smooth and soft. The small birth mark under his ear was still there, just as she remembered. She not only felt so nostalgic, but also cared for. She was still so moved by his presence, even after all this time.

"Remember that field trip to Plymouth Plantation?" he asked, his eye trailing the stars above.

"Which one? We literally went every year from elementary to high school," she laughed, putting a hand on her knee. She pulled the blanket tighter as a breeze rippled through her hair.

"The one during freshman year." Sayer turned his gaze to her, and she grinned.

"Hah! How could I forget?"

Marblehead High, Freshman Year, October 2005

As the whole grade lined up and started walking outside to the busses, Isla could feel the chill of the October air against her cheeks. The sun was slow to rise, making it a little darker than usual. The fog still danced among the tree line around their school, adding to the ambiance of the season.

"All right guys, our class and Mr. Fitmoore's class will be together here on bus twelve. Find a seat and stay there. It's a little bit of a drive, so we don't care who you sit with as long as you're not singing one of those annoying bus songs," her English teacher laughed. Mrs. Parks was about thirty-five and had probably been to Plymouth Plantation a million times. Isla enjoyed her teacher's sense of humor, but also her willingness to understand the trials and tribulations of a high school teenager.

"Isla! We can sit together!" Kelly shouted, making her happiness known to the rest of the class.

"Isla, sit with me," Kelly shouted, peeking over the heads. "Back?"

Isla weaved through the crowd. "Lead the way."

"Did you bring your headphones?" Kelly asked, holding up her iPhone.

"Right here." She pulled them out of the front pocket of her jeans, "I made a playlist for us with all the throwbacks, so let me know if you have one you want me to play."

Kelly nodded, already leaning back and closing her eyes to listen.

They didn't need to talk or gossip for the next hour or so. They were totally content with sitting beside each other sharing a headphone, listening to the same music. That's how you could tell you were someone's best friend.

They sat in silence as the songs went by and the landscape changed around them, showing off the beauty of autumn through cranberry bogs and fallen leaves. Isla saw it all over the shoulder of her best friend, wondering what more she could ask for in life.

"Hey, could I use your hotspot?" someone asked, tapping her shoulder.

"What?" Isla said, turning around.

A boy with a dark gray hoodie and sleeves rolled carelessly up by his elbow was leaning close to Isla over the seat of the bus. He held up his device. "Would you mind if I used your hotspot? My music is having trouble connecting."

"Oh, uh, yeah, I think so," she stammered.

He smiled, his blue eyes shining in the morning sun that had decided to finally find their way through the clouds. "I'm Sayer, by the way."

Isla flushed. She knew who he was. "I'm Isla," she smiled, her eyes lingering on him before turning to her screen. She held it up for him. "Here's my password."

As he was typing into his phone, she noticed something she hadn't before. She knew him from going to the same school, but she wasn't sure she ever really *noticed* him. He was attractive. A strand of his dirty blonde hair fell across his face, tracing a line down to a small birth mark under his ear. Isla stared at him as he typed.

His own eyes barely looked back at her as he folded into his seat. "Thanks, Isla." His cheeks curved around his dimples.

Isla turned around, but the beauty of fall was now masked by her fascination with the boy behind her. Her back prickled as she was increasingly aware of his presence, and it took all her strength not to steal another look at the boy with eyes as deep as the sea.

Why hadn't she ever noticed him like this before? Why did she instantly feel so moved by him?

Sayer was grateful Isla couldn't see him staring at her.

She sat before him, completely unaware of his thoughts on her, and had likely forgotten about him the moment she turned her back. His heart raced as he tipped forward to catch one more sniff of her sweet perfume.

Something about her awkwardness and the innocent air about her drew him in, and just like that, he was ensnared. A slow smile drew across his lips. She was going to be important to him. He could feel it in his bones.

The bus stopped and Mrs. Parks stood up. "Alright class, you know the drill. As you walk around the grounds, make sure you are filling out this worksheet. It is due as soon as you come back to the bus. Remember, it's a grade!" She handed slips of paper to her students as they walked off the bus.

"Do we have to?" some of them groaned.

"Yes, I know it's just so painful," she joked.

Isla and Kelly grabbed their worksheet and headed toward the archway of the entrance of Plymouth Plantation. This recreated 17th Century English Village, modeled after the similar small farming and maritime community that the Pilgrims lived along Plymouth Harbor, was precious. The tiny timber framed houses were homes to villagers and their livestock. These homes were furnished with similar things the colony would have had many years ago. Here, students could freely walk around, talking with costumed role players who were portraying actual residents of Plymouth County, real names and all. It was crazy how on point their acting was.

"Do you smell that?" Kelly asked, pointing in front of them. "A fire."

The leaves crunched beneath their feet as they approached. Around them, colonists fed their livestock, churned butter, and hung wet clothes on a line outside.

"I could have totally lived here," Kelly smiled.

"Umm, no you couldn't, Kel, they didn't have electricity or running water back then. Forget about toilets and showers," she smirked.

Her friend's face pinched together. "Eh, maybe you're right."

The girls walked ahead, students filling up and running around already. The morning dew was shining on the grass while ducks and chickens were perusing the walking path.

"You think they would notice if I caught one?" Isla heard a student ask.

"I dare you to try," another voice insisted.

*Weirdos,* Isla thought.

"Let's go to that house and ask the first question on our paper." Kelly held the paper in front of her.

Someone chuckled behind them. "Kelly, you could probably answer these without even asking, we've been here so many times."

Isla's head whipped around at Sayer's voice. His own paper was folded in his pocket, and he kept pace with them. That same tingly feeling as from the bus made its way across her skin.

"You're probably right," Kelly said, folding her paper up. Her attention didn't stick to Sayer like Isla's did.

"I mean, do you think Mrs. Parks is really going to look at these?" Sayer went on. "Read the first one."

*"What are your daily chores?"*

"Oh, we could totally make these up." Isla said as she scanned the rest of the questions.

"Right," Sayer smiled.

"Whatever," Kelly rolled her eyes and picked up her pace. Sayer fell back, and Isla cast him another look before catching up with her friend. She kept tabs on his presence, though, as they moved throughout the day.

As he ducked inside another house, Isla tugged on Kelly's arm. "Should we go to the Patuxet?"

"Because Sayer's there?"

Isla paused, and Kelly barked a laugh. "Please. You've been staring at him all day. You clearly like him."

"I don't even know him," Isla mumbled.

"We've been in the same class since first grade. He's a bit of a class clown, but he's a nice guy to everyone. You could like worse people," she explained, shrugging.

Sayer slipped outside and Isla turned her gaze. "So, want to come over to my house tomorrow night?" she asked Kelly.

"Sure, I mean my calendar is *wide* open," she said. "I've got to go to the bathroom. You?"

"I'm good."

Her friend took off and Isla glanced back to Sayer. He was looking at her. Their eyes met at the same moment, and she blushed.

Sayer glanced to Kelly as she walked away, then strode to Isla.

"May I join you?" Sayer smiled, shoving his hands in his pocket.

"Sure. Kelly just left to go to the bathroom," she stammered.

Sayer took a deep breath, looking like the picture of calm as he walked down the trail with Isla. "It's an exciting day in the pilgrim town." He gestured to women as they churned butter, and Isla laughed.

The sound of her laugh faded, and a strange silence filled the gap between them.

"So, you play soccer?" Isla asked, already knowing the answer.

"Yes, have been since kindergarten . . . I think," Sayer said. "Do you play any sports?"

"No, but I'm on the school newspaper. I created the column where I review local restaurants and movies in the movie theatre."

"Really? That's you?" he laughed, turning his whole body as he walked to face her.

She ducked. "Yup, embarrassing maybe, but I love to write."

"What is your favorite thing to write?"

"Poetry. Do you like to read?" she asked.

"Not at all," he confessed. "Never really got into books."

"You're missing out. I can just get lost in the characters sometimes."

"Well, maybe you'll have to tell me what to read." His eyes twinkled like he'd just invited her to be part of some exciting mission.

"I can do that," she said, just as Kelly rejoined with them.

Sayer's conversation was polite, but he hadn't joked with Kelly like he had with Isla, and his eyes hadn't lit up when he looked at her.

On the bus ride home, Sayer took a seat next to Isla, and they laughed the whole way back.

## Chapter 8

Marblehead, June 2014

"Isla dear, can you set the table for dinner tonight? Add three more table settings as well, we are having a few guests. Oh, and use the expensive china," Patrice asked Isla as soon as she walked through the door.

"Tonight?" Isla asked, hanging her purse on the hook in the mud room.

"Yes. Make sure you do it soon. They are set to arrive in one hour for appetizers and drinks."

"Who's cooking?" Isla poked, knowing quite well her mother always hired someone if it was more than their immediate family.

Her mother looked up from her stack of papers on the kitchen island. "Polly," she said. "Will that be all right?"

"Thank God," Isla snickered as she wound up the stairs.

Her mother called up after her. "And please shower, dear, your hair looks greasy."

Isla frowned, checking the clock. "Can I do that after dinner?"

"No, do it now." Her mother turned another page without looking back.

Isla found her reflection in the bathroom mirror and ran her hands through her golden blonde hair. She figured she could take a long shower, putting off her chore until right before the guests arrived, which irritated her mother. When Patrice instructed you to do something, you had to do it right then; if not, she would grow increasingly tense. Isla loved watching her mother squirm.

After her long shower, she slipped on a dress. Whoever was coming over must be important. Polly only cooked on big holidays or when her family wanted to impress someone.

As Isla was finishing curling her hair, her mother screamed up the stairs, "Isla, let's go. I gave you *one* job."

"Coming," she smiled, her antics going according to plan.

As she was walking down the stairs, Isla's nostrils were filled with the savory aroma of butter, onions, and garlic simmering. Polly was from the South and absolutely adored butter. Everyone's stomachs would feel entirely too full whenever she cooked.

"Isla!" Polly waved a spoon at her. "How's my college graduate?"

Isla and Polly were close. She taught Isla how to cook over the years, slowly but surely. As Polly cooked, she would listen to Isla and offer her sage advice on dating, friends, and schoolwork. She listened more to Isla than Patrice.

"Good, not too bad. Gearing up for my move to New York in a few months. Do you know who's coming over?" Isla asked Polly.

"I think a client of your fathers, his wife, and their son. Only three this time. Your mother told me about you moving New York. Lots of people there, such an exciting time," she winked.

"Guess that's not too bad," Isla sighed, reaching for the plates. "But I'm there for work. I don't think I'll have much time to do anything else."

"I can set the table, love," Polly offered.

"You know if I don't do it, my mom will freak," Isla said, grabbing six forks and six knives.

"True." Polly turned back to her pot. "Well, I hope you find time to go to fancy parties and meet tons of people. You need to get out of this little town to spread your wings for a bit. Getting out of your comfort zone is never a bad thing."

"That should be on a fortune cookie," Isla rolled her eyes, smiling, "What are you cooking for us tonight?"

"*Duck a l'Orange,*" Polly peeked inside the oven, letting out a new roll of scents.

"That's my mom for you, always making it fancy," Isla said, putting out the plates.

"You have to have some ounce of class, Isla. How else will we help close your father's deals?" Patrice stated, walking through the kitchen to grab a large wine glass.

"How long has that pinot noir been out in the decanter, Polly?" Isla motioned toward the wine.

"Not long, ten minutes, ma'am. Should be ready."

"Good, thank you, Polly," she said, pouring herself a glass. Her hair had been tightly curled, and she wore the fancy blazer, even though Isla knew it pinched her shoulders.

Isla glanced to the door. "Who is coming over tonight?"

Patrice patted a finger against her lipstick. "Your father's clients. Mr. and Mrs. Williams, and their handsome son, Walker." She leveled her daughter with a stern look. "You will be nice to them and on your best behavior. They are looking to buy that old Marina boat storage down by the harbor. I think Mr. Williams wants to turn it into a brewery or restaurant." She waved her hand as she took a sip.

"I would love a glass, thank you, Mom," Isla stated facetiously.

"Not too much," Patrice said.

"So, Isla, they have a son who just graduated from Stanford. He too has a business degree." A spark lit her eyes. "He's also single, like you."

Isla's glass lowered from her lips. "Ah. I see."

"Keep an open mind, dear. You never know."

Isla sensed her mother was onto something. She always had some type of plan conjuring up in her thick, dark, up do. Polly winked at Isla as she took a big gulp of wine, the velvety smooth river making its way down to her stomach. She could feel a slight burn as there was nothing in her stomach to soak it up.

The doorbell sang, all three of them staring at each other.

"Isla, stay here. I'll answer the door with your father. Polly, everything smells delicious. Do you have a time yet?"

"About forty-five minutes," she said, opening the oven to peer at the duck.

"Perfect. Ben? Dear? Our guests have arrived!" she called.

"I know Patrice, I have ears," her father smiled, walking past them from his office. Patrice straightened her blazer and smoothed her dress before following after him.

Isla's gaze traced over the show her mother was orchestrating. *The cook, the fancy china, the wine. Check, check, and check.*

Voices came from the foyer, and a nervous knot twisted in Isla's stomach. Nights with her parent's guests were always riddled with fake pleasantries and exhausting smiles. Her mother acted as if her life was perfect and that she adored her family with every fiber in her being. Her father acted as if he was head over heels in love with her mother, always graciously thanking her for slaving away to make a gorgeous dinner.

Isla would just bite her tongue. Knowing the truth made all of it look ridiculous.

Her mother and father seldom spoke and even slept in separate bedrooms. Patrice only spoke to Isla if one of the two needed something. Her mother was not the maternal type. She hired others to care for her house and her child. Isla was convinced that if someone asked her mother what her daughter's favorite color was, she couldn't answer it correctly.

Footsteps navigated to the living room where they would have the usual small talk and sip on alcoholic beverages until dinner was ready. Isla hated small talk.

"Isla, dear, would you come in and meet our guests?" Patrice calmly called into the hallway.

"You won't have to deal with this when you are in New York," Polly whispered, trying to make her feel better.

"I'm sure they'll have their hand in everything somehow," she smirked, holding her wine close to her chest as she walked into the living room.

"And this is our daughter, Isla. She recently graduated with honors from The University of Vermont," her mother adorned, placing two hands on Isla's shoulders.

"Hello, it's so nice to meet all of you," Isla smiled, shaking each of their hands. Their son caught her attention almost immediately.

"I'm Walker," he smiled, holding onto her hand a little longer than his mom and dad had.

"Hi," she said, looking up into his deep brown eyes. His crisp, navy suit stretched over his wide shoulders, and he unbuttoned it to take a seat.

Isla lowered herself into the chair across from him and their parents mingled on the other side of the room.

"Would you like anything?" Isla offered.

"What are you drinking?" He peeked to her glass.

"Just some pinot," she said. "Would you like some too?"

"Sure, I love a good red," he smiled.

"I'll go grab you a glass," she said, standing.

"I can help," he offered, showing off his white teeth. She led him down the hall, searching her mind for something to say.

"So, how was—" they both asked each other simultaneously and then awkwardly laughed.

"How was Vermont?" he finally asked.

"It was pretty . . . cold," she said, finding the wine that her mom left on the kitchen counter.

"Need a glass?" Polly reached for the cupboard. She passed one to Isla.

"Thank you, Polly," Isla whispered before turning back to her guest. "Stanford, huh?"

He leaned against the island, watching her as she poured. "My dad went there, so it's kind of like a family tradition. Didn't really have a choice, to be honest."

Isla glanced toward the living room. "That sounds like me and the University of Vermont," she said.

"Maybe we'll end up making our own decisions someday," he laughed. "What do you want to do?"

Isla passed him the glass, but she made no move to rejoin the parents. "Well, I'm taking over my dad's real estate company in New York in a few months, going to make the big move."

"Really? That's amazing," he said, graciously taking the glass from her.

"I'm also thinking of submitting some of my writing to a few publications up there too," she added.

"Oh, so you write too?" he asked, his eyes widened, and the corner of his lip raised.

"I try," she sighed. "I figured since I'm going to New York, I might as well submit a few things and see what happens."

"I think that's smart." He nodded. "Always good to have options."

Walker turned back for the living room and Isla followed. Her mother's ever-watchful eye trailed them. Her father was in deep conversation with Mr. Williams, probably about their pending real estate sale.

"So, I hear your dad is starting up a brewery?" Isla asked, sitting on the hard burgundy velvet sofa.

"Yes, yes he is." Walker took a sip of his wine. "Oh yeah, this is good," he said, holding the glass up at eye level.

"You like wine?"

"Well, when your parents often take trips up to Napa, you kind of jump on the train," he explained. "I can appreciate a good bottle."

"Oh, you like wine?" Patrice interrupted. Isla hadn't seen her approaching.

"Yes ma'am," Walker smiled, his back stiffening.

"Well then, you'll fit right in!" Patrice giggled. She flashed her daughter a mischievous grin before turning to the others. "Dinner should be ready in a moment. I can lead you to the dining room."

Isla's father stretched his back as he stood, and by the time he started walking, Patrice was in the dining room pulling out chairs. "Isla, Walker, you two can sit right here, across from each other."

Isla's brow scrunched at her mother's forwardness. "Mom—"

"Thank you!" Patrice cut her off.

Isla sighed again and sat. Across from her, Walker was taking his seat, still smiling at her.

"It's no big deal," he whispered.

"I think I know what she's doing," Isla whispered back.

"I don't mind it," Walker confessed. "I'd sit next to you if I could."

Isla smiled and felt a slight burn in her cheeks and her face growing rosier. Walker was handsome, smart, and up to par with her mother's standards. It was just out of character that she felt a certain pull toward him. It was in the way he obviously cared for the people in his life so tenderly that she wondered what it would feel like to be his.

"Tonight, we are so grateful to have possible clients like you in our home," Patrice smiled, holding up her glass. "To new friendships!"

"Here here!" The Williams family clinked glasses with Isla's family.

"Yes, to new friendships," Walker nodded, staring directly at Isla from across the table.

Marblehead High, Senior Year, October 2008

"Gaila, who is Sayer's father?" Isla asked, not looking up from her notebook.

"Did Sayer ask you?" She added some more blue paint to her canvas.

Isla glanced up to be certain she hadn't offended Gaila, but the woman's face was calm as she painted. "No, I'm just being nosy. He brings him up sometimes. I just don't ever know what to say."

"His dad was definitely a special man. Sayer has his eyes." She sighed as she added white to the top of the waves, accentuating the waves peak.

"Does he live around here?" Isla prodded.

"No. He moved away. I think he's down in North Carolina somewhere. He always wanted to become a full-time fisherman."

Isla bit her cheek before mustering the courage to ask the next question. The words spilled out of her mouth. "Why hasn't Sayer met him?"

Gaila's brush lowered. It took her a moment to reply. "Well, his dad was a fragile man. He couldn't support us. He had a lot going on and I just didn't want to make his life even harder than it was."

"So, he doesn't know about Sayer?"

Gaila's lips stretched tight, and she shook her head. "No, he has no clue. One day, I'll tell Sayer everything, and he can decide whether he wants to meet him or not. I will leave that up to him. That's an important decision I want him to make when the times right," Gaila explained, never looking up from her portrait.

Isla wasn't sure she understood Gaila's reasoning. She knew Sayer was growing increasingly curious, but didn't know why she wouldn't be open and honest with her own son the way she was with everything else in life. She believed one's family history was the foundation to one's life. Without a foundation, how was someone supposed to grow and add rooms or people into their lives? She wanted that so much for Sayer but didn't know how to express that to Gaila.

"Hey, Mom?" Sayer shouted from the kitchen.

"Yes, honey?" she sweetly replied.

"What's for dinner?"

Gaila smiled at Isla, laughing off the conversation. Isla was hoping to return to it, but Gaila left the room, placing her paint brushes down gently on the easel. As she was leaving, Isla stood to better see what she was painting.

A young couple walked down a beach, their backs turned. They mirrored the image of Isla and Sayer. The seas looked rough, however, and Isla wondered if Sayer's mom could foresee a rough patch for them ahead. Did she not believe in them? Or did she hope they would work together to overcome any future obstacle? Nevertheless, Isla knew she had to talk to Sayer about their future, soon. Their senior year was moving along fast, college letters showing up in their mailboxes, reminding them adulthood could no longer be dodged.

"Isla, do you want some pizza before we go to the bonfire?" Sayer asked, walking into the sunroom.

"Sounds fine to me." She turned from the painting with as natural of a smile as she could manage.

"Is cheese and pepperoni okay?" Gaila asked, already on the phone with the little pizza shop in town.

"Yes!" they replied in unison.

Later that night, after dinner, they met with their friends.

"You guys made it!" Kelly shouted, jumping off Jake's tailgate, the roaring bonfire heating up everybody's faces.

"Of course," Isla smiled, enveloping her friend in a hug.

"Want a blanket?" Sayer offered. "I know you get cold so easily." He handed her one from his trunk.

"I would love that, thank you." Warmth seeped through her sweater as he placed the blanket over her shoulders.

"Anything for you," he gushed.

Kelly rolled her eyes. "You guys are so cheesy," she joked.

Others from their high school were there but nobody that they were really that close with. Kelly, however, was friendly with everyone.

"You can sit next to me, Isla." Kelly patted the empty spot on the edge of Jake's tailgate.

The fire was surrounded by big heavy logs. Some people had their trucks backed up to the fire, their legs dangling from the tailgate, getting warmed. Sayer didn't have a truck, so he joined the others on the logs, right below Isla's feet. Never too far away. He liked it better closer to the fire anyway; it made him feel more alive.

Isla's eyes fixed on the bonfire as the embers danced over the kindling. They were so sporadic, never going in the same direction. She suddenly felt like she could relate. Her mind going in a million directions, not knowing where she'd land.

Some days, she wished she could make her own decisions about her future. In a perfect world, she could get a degree in journalism and travel the world, documenting everything she encountered in her small leather-bound notebook. Other times, she just felt like caving into her parents' wishes and attending the University of Vermont and graduating with a business degree, taking over the family's real estate business in New York, and living a secure life.

She wanted adventure. But she also wanted stability. Eighteen felt too young to know for sure which path to take.

How was she ever going to decide? How would she know she was making the best decision? She wanted to be with Sayer, so badly. But she could feel herself slowly pulling away. Was he preventing her from meeting others? She loved him with all her heart, but she felt she wasn't old enough to fully comprehend her own heart. The enraging battle inside intensified with each passing day. As she stared at the fire before her, she couldn't help but sigh. Their love was like a flame, their light slowly fading, succumbed to the oxygen feeding their souls.

"So, Isla, any plans after high school?" Jake asked.

Isla looked up, still deep in thought, "Me?" she asked.

"Yeah, what do you want to do?" he repeated.

She bit her lip. Had he read the battle in her mind? "I don't know. My parents are pushing business school at Vermont, you know, family tradition," she explained, shrugging, trying not to let the uncertainty in her heart spill through her words. "I'll probably apply and see what happens."

Sayer's head turned quickly, now staring upward at Isla.

"Oh, I see," Jake said.

"She doesn't really have a choice," Kelly insisted.

"I think she does," Sayer interjected. He frowned.

Everyone's head turned to Sayer who looked only at Isla. "I think she can do whatever she wants. She loves writing. She should be able to study journalism and travel like she wants to. Why does she have to study business? Because that's what her parents did?"

"Well, babe, they are paying for it," Isla explained. She shifted under so many eyes.

He shrugged, turning back to stare into the fire. "And you just sounded exactly like your mother." Irritation rolled through his tone. "You have a choice. You don't have to do something you hate just because your parents are holding money over your head."

"No, but it's easier," Kelly said. She squeezed her friend's hand.

"Nothing worth having comes easy," he said, glancing back at Isla.

Isla grew embarrassed, grabbing a beer from Kelly's cooler.

"I think it's my choice and whatever happens, happens," she said, twisting off the beer cap and taking a swig. The cold beer fizzed down her throat.

"You'll do great at whatever you decide," Kelly said, raising her glass to Isla.

"What about you, Kelly?" someone else asked.

As everyone else went on with their own conversations and plans, Isla stared at Sayer. It was abundantly clear that they had a lot to discuss.

As the fire fizzled, more and more people were leaving. Nobody wanted the job of extinguishing the fire, however, and it was becoming obvious it would be Isla and Sayer staying.

"So, guess we should talk?" Isla started, sitting on the log closest to the fire as the night sky shone brightly above them.

"Apparently things have changed," Sayer shrugged, sitting next to her.

"Of course, I want to be with you. I just don't know how I'm going to balance everything," she explained. "Vermont is far away. We'd have to be long distance."

"I wouldn't mind waiting for you." His voice was quiet, and his eyes fixed on the last of the bonfire light.

Isla placed a hand on his arm. "I wouldn't expect you to do that."

Sayer threw up his hands. "Well then, what's going to happen? We're just not going to be together if you decide on Vermont?"

Isla just wanted to freeze time. She wanted her two lives to mesh into one. This battle only had one winner, and she knew, deep down, who was going to win.

"I'm not sure. But what I know now is that I love you," she said, taking his hand and looking into his eyes, hoping that above all else, he knew that.

"I love you too, Isla. I hope you always remember that." He pressed her hand to his lips, holding tight as if she might float away if he let go.

As they both looked up at the clear night sky, they each saw the stars, shining brightly. Sayer glanced over at Isla, a single tear rolling down her cheek.

# Chapter 9

Beaufort, August 2019

"John? You here?" Sayer called out.

Silence.

"Umm, John?" Sayer yelled out again, a little louder, this time stepping into the old blue lobster boat.

"Yeah, yeah I'm here. What are you yelling at me for?" he exclaimed, coming out from the trunk cabin.

"What were you doing over there?" Sayer asked.

"Adding some gasoline," he quickly replied, holding a bottle of Jim Beam.

"Yeah, right," Sayer laughed, pointing to the bottle.

"Oh this? I keep emergency gasoline in here just in case." He waved the bottle like it was nothing.

Sayer chuckled. "It's noon. But I won't tell nobody."

"Would you stop your yacking and get to work?" John set the bottle down.

"What do you need done today?"

"Well, the washboard needs cleaning, and the platform over here needs to be repaired." Sayer now noticed the damage.

As they began to work, the bright Carolina sun shone down on them. John's skin was a reddish tan, something he attributed to his Hungarian genetics. Sayer was starting to become bronzed as well, and he always worked without a shirt on. When he got too hot, he would jump in the water to cool off.

"So where did you say you came from?" John asked.

"Marblehead," Sayer answered.

"Massachusetts?" John quickly asked, stopping in his tracks.

"Yes, sir," Sayer said, not noticing John's disturbance to his answer.

"Ever heard of it?" Sayer pondered. "My mom and I have lived there our whole lives."

"Gaila?" John muttered.

"Yeah, my mom's family is straight from Greece, but she loves New England. Marblehead is kind of like Beaufort, right on the harbor, lots of fishing going on."

John's face grew pale.

As Sayer talked and filled him in on his life, John could not help but think about his past. His young life in Marblehead, and the woman he had left behind.

Salem, Massachusetts, November 1976

Gaila picked up her paintbrush and dipped it into the acrylic paint. As she smeared the colors across the blank canvas, she heard someone, very out of breath, stumble into the private studio.

"John?" Gaila asked, looking up from her painting. "Are you alright?"

"What are you doing here, aren't you supposed to be at work?"

"I have some awesome news!" he said, looking excited, his shaggy brown hair in his eyes. "I got the job, in Beaufort!"

"What job?" Gaila's smile turned into a frown. She knew what he was talking about, but she hoped her aloofness would be a message to John. Beside her, Kat shifted on her feet, keeping her eyes on her statue instead of John and Gaila. Kat was Gaila's closest friend and shared the art studio with her.

John crossed the room. "I told you, the job I applied for, the position at West Marine in Morehead City," he stated, acting as if she should know what he was talking about. "Yeah, well, it turns out this could be the perfect time to start fresh. Start my own life, without them," he explained.

"Well, wait. When did you apply?" she asked, putting down her brush. She shot a look to Kat who slowly backed from the room.

John looked down to his shoes. "About a month ago," he muttered.

Gaila's eyes widened. "John, we've talked about this. You have got to fill me in on these things," she sighed. "Why do you always leave me in the dark?"

He straightened, furrowing his brow. "In the dark? I'm telling you now." His voice raised.

"Yeah, after you've pretty much made up your mind." She picked back up her brush and added angry strokes to the canvas. Her jumbled thoughts were racing a mile a minute.

"Well, I still have to interview," he said. He twisted to see her better. "So, there's a chance I don't get it."

"When is your interview?"

"Two weeks." His head ducked to hers, but she wouldn't meet his eyes.

"What about your parents?" she asked.

"What about them? They never cared about me. Why should I care about them?"

Silence.

"Can you stop painting and just listen to me?" he asked.

Her fingers tightened over the brush. "No, you came in during my studio time. I'm not going to waste it talking about some last-minute life decision!" she yelled, annoyed at his arrogance. "I have a show coming up, and I can't waste any time."

"Well, we can talk about it tonight over dinner, okay?" he said, lowering his voice.

"Fine," she whispered.

As he turned and walked away, Gaila's eyes started to water. He knew she couldn't leave. Her dream was here in Salem, in Boston. She had finally made headway after years of art school, her work starting to make a name for itself. She didn't want to let her dream go, so quickly. What was she to do? Her mouth grew increasingly wet as she felt a wave of nausea come over her.

"You all right?" Kat asked as she slipped back into the room. "You look pale."

"I think I might—" she started, as she turned around to puke into the trashcan next to her.

"Oh my god, Gaila, what's wrong?"

"Everything." She sighed, wiping vomit away from the corner of her mouth, feeling dizzy.

"What if you're pregnant?" Kat muttered under her breath.

Gaila's head snapped up. "What?" She thought they had been careful, but who could really know?

"Who just throws up out of nowhere?" Kat asked. "Plus, you've barely been eating."

Gaila went quiet. Kat rubbed her back a few times before returning to mold her sculpture. After a moment, Gaila threw herself back into her painting, her mind racing. She didn't want to even entertain the thought, but it was a possibility. Was she ready for such a commitment? Was John ready? He's now hell-bent on leaving this town to start back up in another. They both have no money. How were they going to support themselves—let alone a baby? Gaila's family, her support system, was in Salem. No way was she going to leave now, especially if she could be pregnant.

She decided that she was going to put all this doubting to rest and take a pregnancy test after her session at the studio. She didn't like to put the cart before the horse, so finally knowing would put her mind, and nerves, at ease.

The hours ticked by until Gaila could wait no longer.

"You leaving?" Kat asked, wheeling her sculpture over the corner.

"I think so, kinda tired." She shrugged, folding her cleaned painting brushes in her leather carrier.

"How tired?" Kat snickered.

"Oh my gosh," Gaila laughed, "as tired as I always am at four in the afternoon."

"Well, I'm just saying," Kat joked.

As Gaila walked home, she couldn't help but tune into her body. The cold air danced around her ears, making her nose twitch. She walked along the harbor, staring out into the sea as the sun slowly make its way back home beneath them. The fall leaves crunched at her feet as she walked along the path, nobody else in sight.

She put a trembling hand beneath her stomach, feeling slightly optimistic.

*What if?* she thought. *What if there is a little miracle inside of me? Rolling around, the size of a poppy seed.* She turned the corner and headed for the drug store. There was only one way to find out.

An hour later, Gaila stood in her bathroom, flushing the toilet and placing the pregnancy test on the counter. She sat on the floor with her back against the cold, white-tiled wall. Her feet crisscrossed at her ankles, and her hands cupped together.

*Three minutes.*

She could hear the dishwasher downstairs running, the wind picking up outside as the evening approached. Cars honking, everyone's lives moving right along except for hers, it seemed. She knew it was close to the three-minute mark, her nerves growing inside of her.

*What will I do? Should I tell John?*

He couldn't handle anything else; his divorcing parents have taken up all of his attention.

She would need to stay in Salem, near her parents and family.

*Support?*

She would need their support.

Gaila stood, looking down on the counter.

*Pregnant.*

Two weeks later, the couple met outside Wale's Coffee Shop in Salem as John was preparing to leave for his interview in Beaufort. Yellow leaves showered them as they stood outside the café, John holding her hand. Fall had quickly approached its peak. Rain clouds were slowly coming in from the bay, and they both knew they didn't have that much time to talk outside.

"Please come to Beaufort with me if I get the job there . . . please. It will make our lives so much easier."

She pulled her hand back. "I've told you before, John, I refuse to follow anybody. Especially a man."

"You're not following me, love. We'd be moving there together."

She motioned to the streets around them. "I want to stay here. My family and friends are here, and I love this small town. I've never left, and I have no desire to up and leave now. That's my final answer." Her jaw set and her lips pursed.

John ran his hands through his hair, staring at the girl he loved. "Really? That's it? You won't even consider it?"

"No," she muttered. Her eyes didn't waver from his, and he took a step back.

"My plane leaves in two hours. I can't be late for my interview."

"I'm not sure why you even applied in the first place?" Gaila said, throwing up her hands.

"It's a lead fisherman job. It pays pretty well, right on the harbor in Beaufort. It's a small town, too. You never know. You might like it," he enticed, searching for anything that might change her mind.

"How about you see if you even get the job first and you let me know."

She turned and walked away, her heart heavy and tears welling.

The past five years they had been together was nothing short of a dream for Gaila. However, it grew entirely too clear to her recently that John was not ready for adulthood just yet. They had just turned twenty-eight, their birthdays just days apart from each other. Gaila was a budding artist in Boston, taking the train from Salem every day. She worked in a small studio with another artist, Kat, waiting tables at night to help pay the rent. John worked as a mechanic on all types of boats at the Safe Harbor Marina in Salem. The pay was decent, but nothing that could support a family.

On a whim, John had applied for the lead fisherman position at the Morehead City Marina in Beaufort, just to see if he would even get a call back. When he did, everything changed. He figured with his new salary, he could afford a small apartment in downtown Beaufort, a perfect two bedroom place for him and Gaila. He felt, with her adventurous spirit, that she would be all for it. However, he did not anticipate her unwillingness to join him. He knew how much she loved to travel, how much she wanted to see the world.

Was it him she didn't want to spend the rest of her life with?

She never could come up with a clear answer, never fully committing. She seemed to have one foot in the relationship—with the other still out.

# Chapter 10

Marblehead, June 2018

"Isla, dear!" Patrice yelled up the stairs to her freshly minted college graduate.

"Yes?" Isla said, walking down the stairs.

"Your father is leaving soon; you will be leaving with him," she instructed.

Isla groaned. "Why do I need to go to his meeting?"

"Because you are soon moving to New York to maintain our family's business, and you need to learn as much as you can before we send you up there all by yourself," Patrice explained, helping Isla button her black pea coat.

"I can handle it. I passed my real estate test."

"Yes, but real-world experience is more productive than just passing a test," Patrice assured her daughter. "You ready?" Patrice asked, walking into the foyer.

"Who are we meeting again?" Isla asked, honestly forgetting the purpose of this meeting.

"Robert Williams, he wants to buy the old Marina boat storage complex by the harbor, remember? They were here for dinner the other night, honey. We are meeting him at the complex to do a walk through and hopefully he will be making an offer. I want you to come to see how deals are made." He exchanged a look with his wife.

"I believe his son will be there as well," Patrice finished.

"Walker?" Isla asked, trying to hide her shock.

"Why yes, yes, Walker will be there as well. His father wants him to learn a thing or two."

"Oh, how wonderful!" Patrice smiled, winking at Isla.

"Mom, I don't want to—" Isla started.

"You'll have a ball!" she said, turning her around and shooing them both out the door. "Go make a deal!" she called after them.

Isla and her father walked over to his sleek, black Porsche SUV. "You can sit up front, sweetie," Ben said, opening the door for her.

"Thanks dad," she smiled.

After getting into the car and putting her seatbelt on, her father climbed in right behind the steering wheel.

"Ready?" he asked.

"I guess so."

As they drove up the driveway and out onto the street, the sun started to show off the beautiful scenery surrounding them, its beautiful rays shining their way down the road.

"Dad, do you think Mom is planning all of this?" Isla asked.

"Planning what?" His smile gave him away.

"Walker. She isn't being very subtle," Isla said, turning on her heated seat.

"Your mother just wants you to be happy. I know that's hard to see sometimes," he explained, taking off his driving gloves.

"I know, but Walker's family seems so stiff," she said, looking out the window.

"They might be 'stiff' at first, but Mr. and Mrs. Williams are lovely people."

The jazz music slowly filled up the silence in the car.

Isla wasn't sure how to handle herself. She thought Walker was nice, and extremely good looking, but that always meant there was something else wrong. She wanted to stay coy, but seem interested. She figured she could do that; it couldn't be too hard.

"Ready to do this thing?" her dad exclaimed, parking the car.

"It's all you, Dad," she said, opening her door and stepping out onto the gravel.

The harbor was so beautiful this time of year. The snow was eminent, but not cold enough. The trees were bare, their leaves laying on the ground like cold, stiff bodies. Lifeless, yet so beautiful in their own right. They didn't have to be filled with color to be beautiful. It was in this stage of grief that they seemed their true selves, awaiting the moment to be rejuvenated again. The spring seemed so far off, but the anticipation of warmer days excited her.

By then, she will be frolicking the streets of New York, selling properties in the upper East Side, enjoying fancy cocktails with her fancy friends. At least, that's what everyone else thought was going to happen. She knew it would never be that easy.

"Mr. Williams, so glad you could meet us," her dad said, shaking Mr. Williams' hand.

"Not a problem. I am excited to look around. This property hits all the things on my list." He stepped out of the way as his son came forward. "You remember my son, Walker."

"Hello sir," Walker smiled, firmly shaking Ben Wade's hand.

The firmness of their handshake did not go unnoticed by Isla, her dad seemingly impressed.

"Yes, Walker, hello again. You remember my daughter, Isla?" he said, gesturing toward her.

"Hi, Walker. Hello, Mr. Williams. It's a pleasure to see you both again so soon." She extended her hand to both of them.

*Dammit. Did she need to add that "so soon" part? Coy, Isla. Be coy.*

"I asked my daughter to come along so that she can learn as much as she can while she's home. You know, she's opening up the family business in New York in a few short months, so being exposed to as many listings as possible will only help her in the long run," explained Ben.

"Of course, we totally understand that. We too would like Walker here to possibly extend this brewery up North. He needs as much exposure as he can get," Mr. Williams added.

It seems as though Walker and Isla had similar lives. All trying to live up to their family's expectations, their hopes and dreams, without giving them any room to make their own decisions. Isla's gaze stayed on him as he followed his father around the lot.

"All right, let's start here," Ben began. "This gravel lot is an ideal spot for parking. So much room!" he explained, pointing to both ends of the "parking lot."

"Hello again." Walker kept his voice low as he paced next to Isla. "I didn't know you would be here."

"I hope that's not a problem," she said, placing her hands in her jacket pocket.

"No, not at all. Just pleasantly surprised," he finished, adding a smile.

"So, a brewery here would be pretty cool. You can't beat the views of the harbor," Isla mentioned, pointing toward the water.

"You sound like a real estate agent." He laughed.

"Well, that is what I'm here for," she said with a grin.

"Fair enough," he winked.

That wink was starting to get to her. Isla could feel herself caving, her feelings for him blossoming. His long legs and broad shoulders seemed to suit him.

"Do you play any sports?" she blurted, not even thinking first.

"Football. I played at Stanford," he said.

*Makes sense,* she thought.

"What position?"

"Quarterback," he said, throwing a pretend football.

"Miss your glory days?" She giggled.

"Actually, sometimes I do," he admitted, his cheeks turning pink.

"Son, look at that view!" Mr. Williams said.

"How could you not notice it, Dad?" He laughed, smiling at Isla.

"Imagine sitting out here with a cold beer on a warm summer day. Breathtaking," Mr. Williams went on.

"It's perfect," Ben agreed. "Especially when everybody is sailing. People could dock their boats and come on up for a snack and a beer. You would have tons of customers," he continued.

"What about in the winter?" Mr. Williams asked. "Would people come sit out here in the cold?"

Isla felt a good idea creep into her mind.

"Oh, yeah!" Isla blurted. "You could have fire pits over here," she pointed, "and people could buy S'more kits and have oyster roasts. I think it would be a ton of fun, especially for the students coming home from college for winter break." She nodded toward Walker.

Ben beamed with pride.

"I love that idea," Mr. Williams crossed his arms as he looked over it all. "You can have something for every season."

"Yes, and you could always install huge glass windows so customers can always appreciate the view in any season," she added.

"You're a smart girl." Mr. Williams pointed at her.

"I've learned from the best." She smiled at her dad.

As they continued to walk the property, Walker stayed close to Isla's side. He asked her questions about her opinions, and listened as she answered. His father seemed interested in her as well, and her dad let her take charge.

"So, when is the big move?" Walker asked Isla.

"Soon," she said with a sigh. "I have to find a place to live."

"Oh?" he pondered.

"Yeah, it's pretty expensive. My dad said he'll help me. I just have to find the right place in the right location. I would love something close to my office."

"Would being next to a new brewery interest you?" he smiled.

She smiled back, now understanding where his mind was going with this.

She didn't know how to answer.

As the four of them walked the property, inside and out, the two dads exchanged handshakes, promising a future deal.

"Well, it was nice seeing you again," Isla said, facing Walker and his father.

"It was a pleasure to see you again as well," Walker said, taking his phone out of his pocket. "Maybe we could keep in touch? You know, for business?" He smiled, handing her his phone.

"I guess so. For business," she stated, a small smile showing. Isla took his phone and tapped in her number. As she was scrolling, she couldn't help but notice all the girl names. *He must get around,* she thought.

After saying their goodbyes, everyone walked back to their cars, keys in hand.

"Dad?" Walker asked, standing on the passenger side of the car. "I have an idea!"

"What is it, son?" Mr. Williams asked as he opened the car door.

"What if I open up a brewery in New York instead of Salem? I know we wanted to expand. What do you think?" he proposed.

"When you come up with a good name, you let me know, and maybe we can talk!"

"Sounds good to me," he smiled, getting into the passenger seat. "So, are you going to make Mr. Wade an offer?"

"I think I am. I can't pass this up," he winked.

"I agree," he stated, and they drove off.

A few days after meeting with Walker and his dad, Isla's phone pinged with a text message. She froze.

"What is it?" Kelly said, placing her coffee cup up to her lips.

"Walker just texted me."

"Well, what did he say?" Kelly asked, placing her coffee mug back on the saucer on the table in front of her.

Wale's Coffee Shop was their go to hangout spot. It was where they went to escape and gossip about what everyone else from high school was doing after college.

"He asked me how my day was going." She held up her phone.

"Well, maybe you should answer?" Kelly insisted.

"I don't know," Isla said, shrugging off the possibility that he might have feelings for her.

"Oh, come on, you haven't been with anyone serious since Sayer. It's time to get back out there," Kelly said. "Do you want a muffin?"

Isla took a sip of her vanilla cappuccino. "Sayer was different."

"How so?"

"He was my person, and so was his mom. I was a part of their family. With Walker, I don't know, his parents are so uppity and pompous," she said, her mouth turning flat.

"Who says pompous anymore?" Kelly laughed.

"Whatever." Isla rolled her eyes. She glanced at the text again. "It's just hard. I can't help comparing everyone to Sayer, even though I know I shouldn't. He was my first for literally *everything*," she confessed.

Kelly squeezed Isla's hand. "I know."

"I haven't opened up again. I don't want to get hurt."

"You can't go into it already wondering how it's going to fail," Kelly offered. "Just go into it thinking he's someone to fill up your time before New York."

Isla chewed on the inside of her cheek for a few moments before picking up the phone. "Yeah, you're right," she said.

"Plus, some free dinners here and there would be nice." Kelly laughed, but her face was completely serious.

"Only you would think that way," Isla chuckled.

The coffee shop was getting busy. The exposed brick and warm fire exuded the old sentiments of Sayer's house with his mom. She wondered what he was up to, how his mom was doing. Was he here in Marblehead? Or had he travel somewhere else? He never seemed like someone to stay in one place forever, and to be honest, she didn't see him anywhere around their small town. She would be lying if she said she never looked around the room at a restaurant she was meeting friends at, searching for him. Sometimes she wondered if he ever saw her, walking around town or driving in her car.

"Well," Kelly interrupted. She leaned forward. "What are you going to say back to Walker?"

Isla's fingers wavered over the screen. "Not sure, how do you think I should reply?"

"You can't seem desperate." She pinched her lips together in thought, drumming her fingers against the side of her coffee.

"What if I just reply *not bad, and you?*" Isla asked, typing it into her phone.

"Oh, I like that. Open the door for him and see how he responds," Kelly said, wiggling her brows.

*Not bad, and you? – Isla Wade*

"Yes, girl." Kelly smiled. "I knew you still had it in you!"

"Oh my god, stop, it's one text message." Her mouth dropped open. "I see the dots popping up already!"

"What? Oh yeah, he likes you!" Kelly beamed.

*It would be better if I could see you - Walker Williams*

"He's totally flirting with me," Isla said, her cheeks turning red as she turned her screen over toward Kelly to read.

"I would say so!" Kelly said. "I'm so proud of you."

Isla rolled her eyes. "I can't text back right away though. I'll give it a few minutes," she said as she took a bite of her now cold blueberry pancakes, placing her phone face down on the table. "It's just for fun, right?" She thought about her first date with Sayer so many years ago.

Marblehead High Sophomore Year, November 2006

"You ready?" Sayer asked, opening his car door for Isla.

"Yes, but where are you taking me?" Her eyes brimmed with delight.

"You'll see. Somewhere fun," Sayer promised with a wink.

They slid into his old navy blue 1984 Mercedes. She loved the smell of weathered leather as she got settled in the passenger seat. She already knew she liked him, but she was excited for what he had planned. Sayer tugged on his sleeves and straightened his shirt many times, so she wasn't alone in her nerves.

"What do you want to listen to?" Sayer smiled, turning the knob on the radio dial.

"I don't mind, just happy to be here." She smiled in his direction.

"Me too," he laughed.

The Eagles filled up the nervous silence between them as Isla looked out the window, her fingers nervously fumbling in her lap. Sayer kept tapping his fingers on the steering wheel, and Isla caught him looking her way as often as he watched the road, finding himself looking at her any chance he could. *She looks so beautiful,* he thought.

He turned into a parking lot outside a teal and cream-painted building with high-ceilings and glass windows to let in the light. "Ice skating?" Isla perked up as Sayer filed into a parking spot.

"You want to?" Sayer asked.

"Of course! I can't remember the last time I ice skated." *Much more romantic than a diner or the movies,* she thought.

"You know, me neither." They both hopped out of the car, making their way toward the entrance.

Sayer felt bold, and as he held open the door for her, he gently grabbed her hand. Isla's heart raced at the touch, and her breathing quickened. It was funny how a thing as simple as holding her hand could illicit the electricity between them.

"Shoe size?" the burly man behind the counter asked.

"Seven for me," Isla said.

"Ten," Sayer said.

They grabbed their ice skates and sat down on the benches surrounding the rink. Cold nipped at their cheeks, and Isla pulled her sweater closer. As they laced up their last shoestrings, Sayer put his hand out.

"Leap of faith?" He held the railing, standing at the cusp of the ice.

"Let's go," Isla placed her hand in his, and he pulled her onto the ice.

Their legs wobbled like a fawn walking for the first time, and Isla clutched Sayer tightly. "Oh, no," she laughed. "This is way harder than I thought!"

"We got this," Sayer said just as his feet fell from beneath him. He plopped butt first on the cold, wet ice.

"You all right?" Isla asked, looking down at Sayer, trying not to laugh.

"Pshh, I'm a pro," Sayer joked.

"Clearly."

Little kids were swirling and twirling around them. They couldn't be older than six years old.

"How are they doing this?" he asked, getting up.

"Not a clue," Isla laughed, offering her hand.

They skated for a while, holding hands and laughing off their occasional falls. Jack Johnson came on the speaker, and everyone's skating slowed, holding hands with their loved one. Sayer's thumb traced slow circles against Isla's skin, and his skating slowed.

In a sudden movement, Sayer twisted in front of Isla and grabbed her other hand. His eyes searched hers, and her breath held in her chest.

"Sayer?" she giggled, her feet fumbling.

"I've wondered what this would feel like all day." His voice was no more than a whisper, filled with tenderness and nervous anticipation.

His hands slid to her waist. His pink nose inched closer to her, and the distance between them closed.

The music of the room quieted as all that remained was the feeling of his lips on hers, his breath warm against her cheek, and his steady hands on her back, holding her close.

This was what perfection felt like.

He pulled away too soon, leaving her yearning for more.

His eyes sparkled like the ice around them, and his smile stretched across his cheeks.

"That was nice," she whispered, failing to find a word strong enough to explain the emotions in her head.

"It was." Sayer laughed.

Warmth spread throughout Isla's entire body. They continued to skate, more slowly now, smiling at each other for the remainder of the hour.

Deep down, Isla knew he would be so important to her.

# Chapter 11

New York, December 2018

There was someone on the street in front of Isla's real estate office. This didn't seem odd, because with the recent opening, there were always people coming and going, whether that be new hires, clients, or lingering project managers making sure their building was in tip-top shape.

"Coming!" Isla said into the intercom, which projected out onto the street. She was still trying to get used to her new office and being the one in charge. Most new hires seemed skeptical at her age, when, little did they know, she had been around this her entire life.

Isla got up from her office chair and straightened her burgundy floral shift dress. Her black heels were a present from her parents, and she was still trying to get used to the height of them. As she approached the door, a familiar face was standing off to the side.

"Walker?" Isla asked, surprised.

"Isla!" He exclaimed, handing her a bouquet of deep red roses.

"What are you doing here? Come on in." She accepted the gorgeous flowers and opened the door wider for him to walk through.

"Those are just for you, a welcome present," he said, walking in. "I know you just began so this will hopefully help you start off your week well."

"Well, they are beautiful," she said, burying her face into the ginormous cluster of roses. "Come on in; my office is this way."

"No receptionist?" he nodded to the empty desk facing the windows.

"Just hired one, actually. She'll be starting next week. Until then, it's just me," she said, leading him down the hall.

Walker's eyes scanned the offices as they walked through. It was adorned modernly with white furniture, sleek black desks, posh light fixtures, and updated laptops plugged in and ready for future agents to use.

"Our new agents are starting this Wednesday, so I'm here getting everything organized and ready for them," Isla explained. She entered her office and motioned to the chair across from her desk.

"It looks great," he said, craning his neck to give the building another look. "I'm sure your dad had a hand in things."

Isla frowned as she searched for a hidden meaning in his words. "He did," she said slowly. "But I had all the creative design ideas."

"Well, it seems that way," he stated, folding his hands, looking out the window onto fifth Avenue.

Awkward pause.

"So, what brings you here? To New York?"

"Actually, I'm starting up a brewery in Times Square," he smiled, resting forward on his elbows. "It's the first extension of me and my father's in Marblehead, as you remember."

"Yes!"

"I'm obviously in charge of this one, but it's finally all coming together."

"What have you named it?" Isla asked, her eyes widening.

"Time Hopp." Walker smiled.

"I love it," Isla answered. "Your idea?"

"All me," Walker laughed. "Surprisingly."

"Well, you're pretty witty," Isla said as butterflies swirled in her stomach.

"Well, our opening day isn't for another month or so, but I've got a place in town, in preparation," Walker explained. "I'm pretty busy with meetings these days in anticipation of our opening. But I was wondering if you'd be interested in going out to dinner this week, maybe tonight or tomorrow?"

The butterflies went wild, and Isla tried to still them long enough to look through her calendar.

"Umm yeah, I'm free tomorrow night," she said. Eagerness spilled through her tone.

"Great," Walker said. "How about we go to this little place I know, Fraunces Tavern. The food is great, and the wine and beer selection is wonderful. They have live music most nights. I'll make a reservation."

"Wonderful." Isla put it into her calendar, "I'll meet you there at . . . ?"

"Six-thirty?" Walker asked. "And I can pick you up. Just text me your address."

"Sure," Isla said, not expecting that.

"Well, Isla, I hope you have an amazing day and enjoy those roses," he said.

"You too," she said. "Let me walk you out."

As they were walking and now standing at the door, Walker leaned in and kissed her on the cheek. "Looking forward to seeing you," he said, squeezing her elbow and walking out. The cold air billowing in, slapping Isla in the face.

"Bye," she stuttered, not sure what had just happened.

Isla turned and smiled. The last time they had talked, she wasn't sure how he felt about her. She also didn't know he was going to be here with her in New York. He mentioned being up north, but Isla didn't think it meant this far north. She figured it would be a good idea to go to dinner and drinks, nothing crazy, just a casual dinner with a friend.

Except that kiss on the cheek. *Is that common?* She didn't think New Yorkers, even New York transplants, were that friendly. *Is he insinuating something?*

It wasn't smart to worry herself about any of this when new agents were starting in a few days, so she put her energy toward that and tried not to dwell on the possible date with Walker.

Isla dove into her work, headfirst, not realizing it was eight in the evening.

*Ugh*, Isla groaned. After packing up, turning off the lights, and securing the security alarm, it had finally hit her—looking back at her clean, polished, now ready office—that she was now a New Yorker, and her family had trusted her to do this job.

She promised herself, then and there, that she would work tirelessly to secure their trust and to work as hard and diligently as she could. After all, she was the one in charge.

As she walked home to her apartment complex on Fifth Avenue, she realized she had been here several weeks without checking her mailbox. Rounding the corner, and walking through the elegant archway, she turned toward the mailboxes nearest elevators and placed her key in box 605. Upon opening the small golden door, she noticed a single letter, sitting alone.

*To: Isla Wade*

*From: Dad*

Isla smiled, placing the envelope under her arm, pressing the elevator key. As hectic as the past few weeks had been, preparing the office and her apartment, she was looking forward to her father's letter.

He could have easily called her, but being old fashioned, nothing got through to her more than his letters. She had kept a box of them underneath her bed. A plethora of birthday cards, well wishes, and of course these long letters when she had accomplished something he was certainly proud of.

The elevator door creaked just a little. She stepped out into the hallway, the fake gas lights illuminating the hallway. They adorned each apartment door, giving it a more intimate feel. This place was far from home, but she appreciated the little things that made it feel that way.

After dropping her keys in her small ceramic bowl, she slid off her heels and hung her purse in the hallway. Her timed, fake candles were flickering on her mantle already. She grabbed a big wine glass and filled it up, sitting on the couch with her dad's letter in hand.

*Dear Isla,*

*I am so proud of the woman you have become. You have done everything right, always putting your energy in the right places, being the hardest worker in the room. I know this was a huge move for you, but you have done so with grace. There is nobody I would trust, other than you, to take my place in this company. You may have big shoes to fill, but just remember, they are yours now. Be tough, but be caring and kind. If you can master these things all at once, your agents and clients will trust you with their sale.*

*You got this, baby girl, and good luck!*

*Love, Dad.*

She placed the letter on the coffee table, laying her back against the couch. This would be a difficult week.

An unexpected name flashed through her mind. *Sayer.*

What would he be thinking? She thought for a second and knew that if he were here in New York with her, he would be making spaghetti with too much cheese and filling up her wine glass. She knew he wouldn't have agreed with her taking over her dad's company. He always told her she was destined for more than just that. Maybe she'd be writing, maybe she'd be interning with the *New York Times.*

She paused and expelled all those thoughts because they simply shouldn't matter. She was starting her life, in her little studio apartment, without him. If he had cared, he would still be a part of her life. She thought of days when it ended with Sayer, just a few weeks before she left for the University of Vermont.

Marblehead, August 2008

*Want to meet up for coffee at Wale's?—Sayer*

Isla looked down as her phone vibrated, distracting her from the mounds of clothes and luggage scattered about her room. Packing for college shouldn't be this hard.

*Sure—Isla*

*How about in 20 minutes?—Sayer*

*Yeah, that's fine—Isla*

Isla got to Wales, grabbing a booth in the corner, one that was secluded, adorned with pictures of fisherman in Salem from the 1600s, and of course from the witch trials. It was their favorite place to sit, the one they always sat in on their dates.

"Hi," Sayer smiled, sliding into the booth, taking his brown corduroy jacket off and placing it at the end of the booth.

"Hey," Isla smiled, biting the inside of her lip as her heart raced and chest heaved.

Sayer glanced over the chalkboard features. "Getting anything?"

"I might grab a latte," she muttered.

"I'll get it . . . vanilla?" he asked.

"Sure, and—"

"Whip cream?" he finished with a sly grin.

"Yes," she whispered.

He knew everything about her. They had spent the last three years together, almost inseparably. How was she going to tell him about her decision? Did he already know? He glanced at her a few times while fetching the drinks, and his mouth was set in a straight line. Her stomach knotted.

Moments later, Sayer returned, handing Isla her latte, extra whip on top.

"Thanks," she said, taking a sip.

"You got some whip cream," he smiled, motioning her to wipe the top of her lip.

"Oh," she said, wiping her lip with a napkin.

Awkward silence filled the booth while they both looked around. The shop was pretty barren. *Good,* Isla thought. *No audience.*

"I think I know why we're here," Sayer started. He held his coffee with both hands.

"You do?" Isla muttered.

He shrugged. "I mean you haven't been acting like yourself for weeks. It's not hard to see you're distancing yourself from me, Isla. Putting this conversation off until today, after I texted you about meeting, it became pretty clear you made your decision."

He was always so in tune with her, their souls tied together somehow. Effortlessly, without talking, they could read each other's body language so clearly.

"I already know you submitted your acceptance letter," he finished. "Without telling me."

The knot curled tighter, squeezing her lungs until it was hard to get the words out. "How?"

"From your mother." He sighed. "It should have been from you, though."

She closed her eyes. "Sayer, I'm sorry." She could feel the blood boil at the sound of *mother*. He knew, out of anyone in the world, the fact that she told him meant that her mother meant to cause turmoil. It was all so clear to her.

"When did my mom tell you?" she asked, baffled.

"The other day, in your kitchen, I was waiting on you to get ready, and she casually let it slip. Oh, and the fact that you chose *early return* on your acceptance letter just makes it that much sweeter."

"Listen, I—" she stammered.

"Oh, I know, you were going to tell me."

"Yes, but—" she tried to finish.

"But when Isla? Tonight? Tomorrow. The day you're leaving? Don't I deserve more than that?" Sayer's voice raised.

"I know you're upset, but can I talk?" Isla said, cupping her warm latte, not caring that it was scorching her fingers. Tears welled.

"Go on then." He folded his arms.

"I did choose return early, but only because I need to find a job. I'm thinking of interviewing for their school newspaper. It pays a good amount, well, a good amount for a student. And I just want to get my life together, get all moved in and ready."

"Without me," Sayer muttered, under his breath.

"What?" Isla asked. "What did you say?'

"Without me," Sayer said louder. "I know you, Isla. You put things off that cause you stress until the very last minute because you don't know how to handle it. You hope that things just blow away, so you don't have to deal with it. Well, guess what? I'm not just something that blows away. I'm your person and you are mine. It's different." His eyes moistened.

"We are different," Isla agreed. "But I need to know that for sure."

"What does that mean?" he asked, clearing his throat.

"I just feel like I haven't been away from this town yet, like I haven't met everyone I'm supposed to meet. I don't know, there's a small part of me that knows I'm supposed to do something more," she said.

"And you are! But is Vermont the answer? Your parents have been telling you what to do your whole life and now you're settling even more by studying what they are telling you to study . . . *business!* You *hate* business and real estate! Unless there is something bigger you're not telling me."

"I don't hate it," Isla said, staring into her drink.

"Well, you don't love it. You'd rather write."

"It's what my family needs . . . it's what my dad will need."

"I just don't know why I don't get to be a part of it, to be a part of you realizing who you can really be."

Isla could feel the lump forming in her throat as two voices in her brain battled it out. On one side, her heart side, she wanted to be with Sayer forever. On the other side, her logical side, she needed to put her own thoughts and feelings aside for the better of her family.

Going to college in Vermont was big, and it was already complicated and confusing. Trying to fit Sayer into that new life didn't feel right. He didn't fit there. He was a part of her life here, the life she was trying to outgrow.

She knew she also had to be honest with him and herself, because there was also a part of her that wanted to meet, and date, other people. She loved Sayer, completely, but how would she know he was the one if she never experienced anyone else? She had to be honest.

"Because I also need to meet other people," she whispered, looking down as a single tear escaped.

"You what?" It sounded like all the air was taken from his lungs.

"Don't make me say it again." She sighed, finally looking up at him.

"You want to meet other people? Like *date* other people?" he asked, dumbfounded.

"How will I know, years from now, if we were truly meant to be?" she said, tears flowing.

"Isla," he whispered, not taking his eyes off her. "Why would you ever say that?"

"It's just been something I've had sitting in the back of my mind, but I can't ignore it anymore. I love you, but what if there is someone else out there that I'll never meet if I'm with you?" She sniffled, pulling her sleeve up to her nose.

"Stop asking those *what-if* questions. Those *what-if* questions are real life," he insisted.

"I can't stop thinking about it. I don't want to resent you years from now," she said. "I would rather miss you than resent you, Sayer."

"Well," he paused. "I guess you've made up your mind about us."

"Sayer—"

"I need to go. Have fun in Vermont, Isla," he huffed, getting up abruptly.

"Wait," Isla said, trying to stop him, sliding out of her seat to follow him.

"Just remember," he said, walking out.

"Remember what?" she asked, in front of the entrance in the coffee shop.

He threw his full cup into the trash and spun around to face her, standing in the middle of the parking lot with red eyes and cracking a voice. "Everything, just everything. Who knows you better in this whole world, Isla?"

She stood, silent, trying to keep her tears at bay.

"I think you're wrong and I won't stay around here to find out," he said, turning his back to her.

"What does that mean?" she asked, watching him walk away.

"You don't get to find that out," he shouted, turning the corner down the alleyway through the town hall.

Isla returned to her seat, her eyes wet with emotion. She knew she was doing the right thing, but it hurt so badly. She could feel her heart breaking, tearing its way through her chest. She put her coffee off to the side.

Just like that, Sayer had walked out of her life, the boy she had known seemingly forever, a boy not fully aware of his own past.

# Chapter 12

Salem, December 1976

It was a Saturday morning, and the art studio usually wasn't open on the weekends, but Gaila had asked Kat for her key.

"I just need to get my mind off of things," she had told her. "I need to put some extra work into my painting."

"Sure, Gail, whatever you need," she said, handing her the key.

"Thanks," Gaila sighed, putting the key in her purse.

"Did you get the news you wanted?" Kat asked. Her gaze dropped to Gaila's stomach.

"I'm not sure yet," Gaila muttered. "I hope so."

As Gaila was squirting colors onto her pallet, she knew this was the right time to be working on her craft. With her emotions heightened, she tended to get more of a dramatic effect completed, and she wanted this piece to be special. She turned on the radio and listened to the melody, curving her brush around each turn.

She became lost in thought—entirely.

She knew John wasn't ready to be a father; his parents would be so upset with him, especially in their own state of destruction.

He was too fragile; she didn't think he could survive the amount of responsibility a child brought into a relationship. If she was honest, she knew he loved her, but he wasn't ready to be a father.

It had become so clear what she needed to do. She wasn't going to tell him; John could never know. If he got the job in North Carolina, he could leave and that would be it. She would be the best mother she could be.

She could do that—provide everything this child needed.

"I got the job," John said, standing outside her apartment as rain poured down behind him.

Gaila looked away from him; she couldn't believe it.

"I leave soon, in the next few days," he explained. "It's a quick turnaround, apparently."

"I see," Gaila responded.

"That's it?" John took a few steps into the apartment, holding out his hands for her.

The television was playing in the background. The hot water in her tea kettle started to scream.

"Let me get that," she said. "Come in."

Gaila walked to the stove, grabbing the handle of the tea kettle, slowly moving it off the burner.

"Earl Grey?" she asked. That was John's favorite.

"No thanks," he muttered.

"I can't come with you," Gaila said, bluntly. "I have too much here, my whole life. I don't want to follow you to North Carolina, John. I just can't."

"I figured that'd be your answer," John replied with a sad nod. "You were never one to change your mind."

"I'm sorry, John. I just can't. It's either we are all in, here in Salem, or not at all."

"I know, it's all right," he said, moving toward her, taking her hands into his.

"A part of you will always be with me though, wherever I go." He smiled, tears welling.

"You too," she said, putting one hand on her stomach.

"I just hope one day our paths will cross again, when it's right."

"You never know," she muttered, wiping away a tear.

"I'll always love you, Gaila. Thank you for being so honest."

*Honest?*

Gaila felt like someone had just punched her in the gut. If anything, she was being the most dishonest she'd ever been. *He's not ready,* she kept telling herself. *This will break him.* If life wanted them back together, they would cross paths once again. At least, she hoped.

"I'll see you," he said, embracing her in a long hug.

"I'm sorry," she whispered, her eyes becoming glassy. "Can we just freeze time?"

"I wish." He patted her back, giving her a single kiss on the side of her head.

They both stood there in the doorway, afraid to move. Once someone moved, their time apart would start.

Distance was a funny thing. It was either a healer or a destructor, taking someone's heart into custody. The two who decided to take that chance knew that it might not end in their favor. Gaila never wanted to take that gamble, and John didn't mind trying. It was there, in that moment, that Gaila knew it could never last. Letting him go was the hardest but easiest decision.

"I'll see you," he said, letting her go.

"Goodbye," she whispered, watching him leave.

Marblehead, March 2020

"It's getting pretty dark," Isla noticed, looking over at Sayer. The sun had set, and dusk approached.

"It got dark pretty fast. Guess it's time to head on in," he said, getting up out of the Adirondack chair, putting the small bonfire out.

"Guess so," Isla said, slowly standing.

"Want to come in? Or are you heading home?" Sayer asked, taking the last sip of his wine.

"I could stay a little longer," she smiled. "This wine didn't help." She laughed, tipping the glass back to reach the last sip.

As they walked up to the back of the house, Sayer could feel his cheeks getting red. He had dreamed of this moment, not thinking it would ever come. He slid open the door and let Isla in first.

"Thank you," she said. "You're still a gentleman."

"Always," he joked.

Isla plopped on the couch, and Sayer went to grab more wine.

"Anymore for you?" he asked.

"Maybe just a little," she teased.

"So, how long are you here for?" Sayer asked, bringing their glasses over to Isla on the couch.

"I think I'm staying a long time," she said.

"Where are you going to live once you sell your parents' place? I mean, you're pretty much homeless." He laughed.

"Oh my god, I am," Isla realized, laughing along with him. "I'll just get a little apartment in town probably."

"I could help you," Sayer offered.

"I would like that," Isla smiled, rolling her fingers through her blonde hair.

"So, does Walker know?"

"I'm sure he's figured it out by now," Isla said.

"Well, if you need anyone to lean on, I'm right here," Sayer smiled.

"Thank you," Isla said, smiling. Her tone had dropped to hardly a whisper, and as he leaned in to fill her glass, she didn't pull back. Their faces grew closer together.

Sayer placed the bottle on the table as Isla glanced down at his lips and then traced up to his blue eyes. Sayer's world stopped as he moved his hand up to her cheek, gently holding her in his hands once again.

She slowly went in, her lips finally on his. Lightning shot through his spine, his heart exploding.

Sayer shifted toward her, his other hand now on her waist. They moved slowly together, kissing each other endlessly. He had waited years for this, the anticipation completely taking over. Sayer continued to kiss her gently, stroking her blond hair away from her face.

"You want to move this to the bedroom?" he whispered.

"Please," she said, staring into his eyes.

For the rest of the night, until dawn, they passionately made love. Entangled in the sheets together, not wanting their dream to end. But it did, and the following day came quickly, bringing with it the grim reality of her father's death.

"Isla, hurry up, this isn't your show," Patrice said, her jaw locked, giving her daughter an angry expression.

"I'm aware of that, mother," she said, rolling her eyes and walking out of the hall bathroom.

"Is this house on the market yet?" Patrice asked, grabbing her purse.

"Yes, it's been listed for a few days now," Isla explained, walking outside to the black limo awaiting them.

"Anyone interested?"

"Not yet. It's a small town, it might take a little longer," she said as the driver opened the door for them.

"Hello, sir," Patrice started. "Can we go by the Harbor Light Inn to pick up another guest?"

"Of course, ma'am," he promised.

"Who else is coming?" Isla asked.

"My mother, of course," Patrice stated.

*Seriously?* Isla thought. This was beginning to feel like a parade.

Patrice Wade was always up to something, always putting the attention on herself. If it wasn't, she would change the conversation to something that related to her, every time there was an opening for it. It seemed her father's funeral was no exception. Patrice didn't have siblings, which was probably a good thing. She would have been too overbearing. She craved attention, especially by her own mother. If her mother was not impressed, Patrice would stop at nothing to achieve it, even at her own daughter's expense.

"Is this all necessary?" Isla asked, taking her seat on the other end of the limo, as far away as she could get from her mother.

"She's family, Isla. Show some respect." Patrice rolled her eyes, checked her lipstick in her compact mirror.

"She hates me," Isla explained.

She snapped the mirror shut. "She does not, and anyway, she's getting older, give her a break."

Isla remembered her younger years, listening in on her mother and grandmother's phone conversations. When Patrice and Isla fought, she was almost always on the phone calling her mother, complaining about Isla. Isla would grab another phone and listen in, noticing all the extra details her mother would add to make her look like an awful person.

Isla took this to heart. She wondered if that was how her mother truly felt about her—

a wedge in her marriage. She always got along with her father the best, but did her mother even want a relationship with her? She never tried. When Isla had wanted to talk with her, her mother would always reply, "Go bother your father." Over the years, Isla internalized the rejection.

She couldn't bother her father anymore. He was gone. And with him, Isla's connection to her mother vanished as well. She suddenly wished, on the way to her father's funeral, that she could finally cut ties with her mother. There had to be a way. She could not live like this any longer. If she was going to cut the negative out of her life, her mother should be number one.

"Oh, we are here," Patrice announced, to just Isla.

"I can see that," Isla murmured.

Watching her mother get out of the limo to greet her grandmother was a sight. Patrice had on a big fur coat, with a mix of real brown and black fur, speckled with white spots. Her grandmother, Ida, had on a similar coat, tanner. They embraced each other with a hug, kissing each other's cheeks. No remorse apparent; no condolences.

"You didn't tell me she was going to be here," Ida exclaimed, getting into the limo.

"Hello, Grandma," Isla said, folding her hands in her lap. "I am my father's daughter, you know."

"Well that you are!" she clucked. Isla could feel the sarcastic jab.

"What time does this event start?" Ida turned to ask Patrice.

*Event?* Isla rolled her eyes as soon as the word sputtered out of her grandmother's mouth.

"The funeral starts at two and should end around three. We'll go back to our house where we will have a catered reception," Patrice said proudly.

"Catered?" Ida stuck her nose up in the air. "I hope you have plenty of food ready for the guests."

"We will, Mother," Patrice assured her.

It wasn't long until the limo pulled up to the gravesite, her father in the casket. The rain pounded on the roof of the limo as the tires rolled to a stop over the muddy path.

"I didn't bring an umbrella," Ida proclaimed.

"Ma'am, I have plenty. I will meet you on the other side," the driver insisted.

Isla stared at the rain droplets falling down the window. Each one seemed to be on its own path, some quicker than others. She felt, in that moment, like a sliding drop of rain on the window of her life. She was determined to get through this day, a day like no other. As her mother and her grandmother exited the limo, Isla could see someone off in the distance holding a single, black umbrella and standing off to the side of their family's tent.

"Sayer?" she whispered.

There was a small crowd gathered by the family's dark green tent, umbrella's covering the rain from most of the guests.

Isla quickly scooted toward the exit of the limo, grabbing the umbrella the driver offered her.

"Thanks," she smiled.

She trudged up the small, grassy hill to her father's gravesite as the crowd turned to greet Patrice, Ida, and her with their deepest condolences. Isla's mother told her to take her seat next to her immediately so they could start the service.

As the priest was talking and reading Scripture from the Bible, Isla glanced over the crowd, their solemn faces making this moment unbearable. She was trying to hold back her tears when she made eye contact with Sayer.

His kind eyes made a safe place for her in that moment. She smiled and let a tear escape, his eyes never wavering from hers.

As the service ended, her family got up and mingled among their guests. Sayer walked toward Isla with his arms extended. The familiar scent of his cologne from the night before swept under her nose.

"It was nice of you to come," Isla said, smiling.

"I wouldn't have missed it," Sayer said.

"Well, thank you," she said, looking over at her mother.

"Do you want to get out of here?" Sayer suggested. "I can tell you're overwhelmed."

He still knew her so well.

"Please."

"Let's go," he said, gently taking her hand in his.

"Where do you think you are going?" Patrice said to Isla, staring angrily at Sayer.

"Hello, Mrs. Wade," Sayer said. "I'm so sorry for your loss."

"Thank you," she murmured, impolitely.

"Mom, I just need some air," Isla said.

"And you don't think I need some air?" her mother huffed.

Isla's lips drew into a thin line. "That's not what I'm saying."

"I see," Patrice murmured, looking at Sayer with her nose up in the air. "Your father's reception is at three-thirty, remember that."

"Goodbye, Mother," Isla said.

They walked toward Sayer's car, her mother's eyes still on Isla.

"That's what you've been dealing with?" Sayer asked, opening the car door for her to get in.

"I wish I had a different answer," Isla admitted as she shook out her umbrella and tucked it near the door.

"Seems like nothing's changed," he said, getting into the driver's seat.

"Where are we going?" Isla asked.

"I know a place," he assured her. "You might remember it."

He started his old Mercedes. Its tan leather seats were worn throughout the years, but the tape player was still intact.

"I remember this thing," Isla smiled. "I can't believe it's still running."

Sayer laughed. "I know, right? I've been keeping up with her, kind of surprised myself. It was at my mom's house in the spare garage."

"Lots of memories in here," Isla snickered, looking at Sayer.

"You're absolutely right." He smiled. "This car could have taken us anywhere."

Isla paused. He wrote that line in her yearbook senior year, back when people still wrote each other notes in yearbooks.

"Yes," she whispered. "It definitely could have."

As they drove, the rain turned into a light drizzle, the gray clouds still taking over the sky.

"Remember this place?" Sayer said, parking the car.

"Old Burial Hill." Isla laughed. "Man, I used to love this place."

"I know," Sayer admitted. "Let's go up to the lookout though, across the street."

They both got out of the car, walking across to the steep steps up toward the historical lookout. As they trudged up the tiny cobble steps, Isla couldn't help but smile. She could start to smell the cool, salty air, and she knew they were almost to the top.

"You all right back there?" he asked, looking behind at her.

"Yes," she giggled, a smile slowly curling.

He reached the final step and turned around, extending his hand and helping her up the last step.

Isla walked past him, staring out onto the vast ocean before them. "It's still so beautiful," she said.

Sayer's gaze remained on her.

"You know he's here, here with you," Sayer said.

Isla took in a deep breath, her lungs contracting and relaxing. A sudden calm washed over her, her tense shoulders falling alongside her body. She closed her eyes, smelling the crisp fresh air. As she stood there for what seemed to be an eternity, Sayer wrapped his arms around her.

"I'm here," he whispered. "It's only us."

Isla fell into him, allowing herself to be held by his arms. His chin rested on her shoulder close to her cheeks.

"I've missed you," she said, a lump in her throat forming.

"I as well," he replied.

"Do you think our paths were supposed to cross again?" she asked, wiping away her tears.

"I'd think it strange if they weren't." He smiled.

"I just need to know the direction I'm going is the right one. Without Dad, I have no clue where I'm going," she sobbed.

"All you need is this heart in your chest," he said, lowering his hand to hover over her heart.

Isla put her hand on top of his. "You know, you're right." She sighed. "You've always been."

"I don't need to be right," he added. "I just believe in you."

They stood there in silence for a while, holding each other.

"Come here," he smiled, turning her around to face him.

Before he could put his arms around her, she stopped him. She stared into his eyes, into his soul. She knew this was the heart she was meant to love. All that time apart was in preparation for this moment, this time in their lives. She realized then, they both needed time to grow up on their own. To become who they really were, so they could continue to grow together.

Sayer, ever so gently, placed his right hand under her cheek bone, his hand extending down her neck. A small chill reverberated down to her toes as she placed her hands on his hips.

"I'm still in love with you, Isla," he confessed, leaning down, their lips touching.

She kissed him back, her soul setting itself free.

A few months after the funeral, Sayer went to his mailbox.

"Hey, love, these are for you," Sayer said, placing a few envelopes on the island in the Airbnb.

"Really?" Isla asked. "How would anybody know this address?"

"Not a clue," he said.

Isla grabbed the two hefty yellow envelopes, looking at the return address, from New York. Opening the first letter, her heart sank.

*NOTE OF ISSUE—UNCONTESTED DIVORCE*

"What is it?" Sayer asked, placing his coffee cup down.

"It's—" Isla paused, reading it again.

"It's divorce papers," she murmured, showing him the page. "From Walker."

"Hmm," he responded, both of their worlds stopping.

"How would he know where I was?" she asked, looking up at Sayer.

"Not a clue," he said.

"When I left, I didn't leave an address or anything, I just wrote him a letter and told him I was leaving him. There's no way he knows I'm here," she said, wearily looking around. "Oh my gosh." Isla's hand flew to her mouth.

"What?"

"My mom," she said, pounding her fist on the table. "Jesus Christ."

She slammed the papers on the floor and walked to the window, looking out at the ocean.

"You think she would out you like that?" Sayer asked, treading lightly.

"Do you know my mother? Yes." She groaned.

"Well, what does this mean? Is there another envelope?" Sayer asked, picking up the papers on the floor.

"Yeah," Isla said, walking over to him.

Opening the letter, she finally pieced together Walker's intentions for their divorce.

*ASSETS*

*100% legal rights of Wade Real Estate Group to the plaintiff, Walker Williams.*

"What the—" Isla was furious now. "He wants my family's real estate company!"

Isla stared at Sayer, her eyes beginning to burn.

"Can he do that?" she asked.

"Well, you are technically still married," Sayer pointed out. "Did you have a prenuptial agreement or something in place to protect your company?"

Isla's stomach felt like it had fallen onto the floor.

"No," she whispered. "He technically owns half." Isla felt like she just got slapped by a brick.

"But the paper says one hundred percent. So, I guess he's wanting to fight for all of it?" Sayer asked.

"Yeah, it looks that way." She groaned.

"I mean, you've been working from here. Has anyone from New York mentioned seeing him?"

"No, everyone's full steam ahead," she noted. "They basically run themselves. They would have mentioned if he had been in the office. He doesn't know real estate like my family did; he's just after my money."

Sayer grew silent, letting Isla process this all on her own.

"It's like this was his agenda all along," she muttered.

"I can't believe he'd do this to me, to my family," Isla pondered, sitting down on the deck out back, overlooking the harbor. "I mean, I can. I left our life in New York. I left him with just a letter," she explained.

"He's not going to make this easy for you," Sayer continued, trying to be supportive. He sat beside her and wrapped an arm over her shoulders. His fingers traced slow circles across her skin until she let out a deep breath.

"I know." Isla sighed, looking down at the divorce papers in her hands.

"How long do you have until you have to respond?"

"Thirty days," Isla said. "According to these papers."

"Are you going to just let him have it? Your company?"

Isla paused, looking up at Sayer. "That's a hard call," she explained. "On one hand, I want nothing more than to erase that part of my life, but it's also the part of my life that has defined me. I mean, moving, all by myself, to a big new city and taking on the challenge of sustaining my family's hard work has been such a momentous milestone for me. However, on the other hand, I want nothing more than to leave it all behind because it brought so much pain," she said, instinctively caressing the now dark purple bruise on her neck from her and Walker's last disagreement.

"Is that what you want?" Sayer asked.

"I want this life," she said, looking around her—the vast open blue ocean, the seagulls cawing above them, and of course, Sayer himself. "In a way, I've always wanted this to be my life."

"I've wanted this too," he confessed.

Isla took a deep breath before responding.

"It's settled then," Isla confirmed. Her passion for Walker soured and she wondered if she had been duped all along. She thought of a night in New York that at the time seemed innocent enough but should have been a warning.

New York, November 2018

"Hello!" the hostess exclaimed as Isla walked into the old Fraunces Tavern.

"Hi," Isla nervously said, gently putting her blonde wavy hair behind her right ear.

"I think there is a reservation, under the name—" Isla started.

"Isla!" Walker interrupted, walking toward her with his arms open, holding a full martini glass.

"Hi!" she smiled, returning his embrace. "Guess I found my party." Isla laughed a small snort, instantly growing embarrassed.

"Have a great night, Mrs. Williams." The hostess winked.

"Oh, no, we're not married," Isla awkwardly said.

"Well come on, our tables this way." Walker gently tugged on her arm. "This place is magic, isn't it?"

The Christmas decorations were in full swing. Fake Fraser fir trees adorned every corner with twinkling warm lights filling the room, creating a warm friendly ambiance.

"It is beautiful," she replied, taking it all in. It wasn't too crowded, but the guests who were there seemed to be enjoying themselves.

"Our table is right here, nestled in the corner," Walker said. "It's my favorite in the house."

He led her to a dark wooden booth, similar to the one at Wale's Coffee Shop back in Salem. She shoved the memory out of her mind as quickly as she could, reminding herself she was starting fresh.

"This is perfect," Isla replied, smiling ear to ear.

Fraunces Tavern was the oldest colonial building in New York City, operating since 1762. Its beautiful interior featured wood from the original structure and everyone who dined there could not escape its charm. It felt like you were thrown back into colonial times, waiting for George Washington to walk in for a beer.

"It's an old place, but I love how they've kept it going," Walker said, taking Isla's coat.

"Yes, I've never been here," she said, freeing her arms from her jacket, watching Walker place it on the hook next to her.

"I know a lot of hidden gems," he insisted. "The beer selection here is not so bad either."

"Well, you would know that." She smiled, getting comfortable in her seat, reaching for the drink menu.

"What shall we start with?" Walker asked, sliding into the booth as well.

"Hmm, not sure, but I think I'm feeling the Rose," she said.

Walker grimaced. "Rose?"

"Yeah," Isla wavered. "Is that okay?"

Walker took a moment to look at the drink menu.

"There's just so much to choose from. Are you sure you don't want something signature?"

Isla wasn't sure how to respond, so she perused the drink menu once again.

"Hello, you two!" Their waitress hovered over them. "Welcome to Fraunces Tavern. Can I get you a drink to start?"

"Yes, I would like a Johnny Walker Black," Walker replied.

"And for you, ma'am?"

Isla looked quickly at the menu again, feeling like she needed to change her mind.

"I'll have the White Smoke Old Fashioned," she said, placing her drink menu face down.

"Lovely choices. I'll be back with some waters and then I can take your orders for dinner. Are we getting food tonight?" she asked.

"Of course, take your time," Walker insisted. As the waitress walked away, his eyes trailed her.

"So, how's the Big Apple treating you so far?"

Isla smiled, as she normally did when anyone asked how she was doing.

"Everything's going well. Amazing city."

"It really is, so much to do and so many people around," he added.

"What made you come here?" Isla asked. "I didn't know the city was the destination you had in mind."

"Well, my dad and I found the right space and we couldn't pass on it," Walker said. "And I needed to get out of Marblehead. I wanted to do my own thing."

"I get it." Isla sighed. "This city is turning out to be the best thing for that."

The waitress interrupted. "Here you go!"

"Oh, thank you!" Isla said, admiring how expensive her beverage looked.

"Yes, thank you," Walker responded.

"Ready to order some food?" the waitress asked, pulling out her note pad.

Walker ordered a filet and Isla a steak salad. She didn't want to go overboard, since she wasn't sure if she was going to be paying for herself. She never liked to expect those types of things. Jazz music filled the room with a sultry single saxophone solo to start the evening.

"So, how's writing coming along?" Walker asked.

"Writing?" she asked.

"Yeah, you mentioned back in Marblehead you wanted to submit some of your poems to magazines?" he reminded her.

"Oh yeah, right. I haven't done that yet, trying to find the time."

"You should find the time and submit some pieces. You never know," he said.

"Yeah, they're just personal. I'm not sure about sharing them yet," she confessed.

"Well, I know there are a ton of lit magazines here in the city. One of them is bound to like your work," he said.

"Maybe," she said, sipping her drink.

"How is it?" Walker nodded at the cocktail.

"Oh this? It's pretty good!" she said, lying to herself and to Walker.

It was sixteen dollars and too bitter for her taste.

As the night progressed, they chatted about future goals and their families, munching away at their expensive meals. Isla found herself asking Walker more about himself than he did of her, causing her to feel exhausted by the time they both finished their meals. She felt she constantly had to be on her game, ready for any comment.

"Ready for the check?"

"Yes, here you go," Walker said, handing the waitress a steel-black credit card.

"Oh, you don't have to do that. I can—" Isla started.

"No, I insist." Walker winked at her, Isla's cheeks becoming flushed.

"Well, thank you," she smiled sweetly at him.

"You're ever so welcome," he laughed. "As long as you will promise to do this with me again."

Isla paused, looking around the restaurant. "Sure," she stated, wondering, *why not?*

"Perfect," he beamed.

# Chapter 13

When John stepped onto the Lobster boat, he had a sense of dread wash over him. He knew his days with Sayer were numbered now that the boat had been restored. And he wanted to do something for the boy, something he wouldn't appreciate until later. He bought a bottle of merlot, native to Beaufort, and hid it in storage with a note that read:

*Share this with someone who made everything worth it. Don't forget our promise. John*

He knew Sayer would find it when he was supposed to.

"Morning, John!" He could hear Sayer stomping onto the boat.

"Hey, did you bring your lunch today?" John asked, poking his head around the corner.

"Nope!" Sayer laughed. "Honestly, I totally forgot to pack a lunch."

"Well, good," he smiled. "It's about time we went out for lunch."

"Oh yeah, where?"

"There's a little place up the way." John pointed.

Moments later, Sayer stood in front of the food truck labeled *Pork and Go!*

"Pork and Go?" Sayer asked hesitantly.

"Oh, hush your whining." John bumped his shoulder.

"How can I help you two?" the owner of the food truck asked. His thick Southern accent boomingly apparent.

"Uhhh, we would like two number one's please," John said. "And yes to the coleslaw."

"Coleslaw?" Sayer groaned.

"Listen, it's a rite of passage, kid."

They both grabbed their sandwiches and headed back to the pier, stopping to sit on a park bench overlooking the water.

Sayer's phone rang.

"Go ahead, son," John said.

"Thanks," he whispered. "Hey, mom!"

John could hear a woman's voice on the other end, always sweet and kind.

"Yes, mom, I'll be back in town for your art show," Sayer promised. "Yes, the eighteenth. It's in my calendar. No, I don't need money to fly up, I got it."

A few moments of conversation went by, John noticing the other boats coming in from the open water. It looked like a storm was leering. *They'll have to end their day sooner than they thought,* John surmised.

"Forever and always," Sayer said.

John stopped chewing the sweet pork that was sloshing around the inside of his mouth, stunned by what he had heard Sayer say.

"What did you say?" John asked.

"Oh, that?" Sayer said, embarrassed. "It's just a saying my mom and I have said to each other since I can remember. She says 'until the end' and I finish it with 'forever and always.'"

John could not believe what he'd heard and nearly choked.

His next thought—*Gaila.* His love some two decades ago.

Salem, November 1976

Gaila turned to John, their last days together dwindling before them.

"Are you afraid to leave?"

"I'm not even sure—" he started.

"Are you afraid to leave for Beaufort?" Gaila asked again, interrupting him.

The leaves were falling around them, and the bench outside the marina boat storage complex was cold yet inviting. The crisp fall air licked their faces.

"Let's sit," John suggested.

They each took their place next to each other on the brown park bench. John extended his arm around Gaila to warm her up, her black pea coat too lite.

"If I decide to leave, I will be somewhat scared," John admitted. "But without my parents and without that drama in my life, I am looking forward to a fresh start."

Gaila winced at hearing him say "fresh start," knowing that she was no longer part of his story.

"You know whatever happens between us, I'll always love you," John said, leaning to kiss her.

"Until the end?" she asked, her swollen red eyes looking up at his.

"Forever and always," he whispered, gently holding her delicate face in his hands. John could feel Gaila's lips trembling.

She wasn't sure if it was the pregnancy hormones settling in or her emotions, but she could not stop the flow of tears.

John was not only choosing to leave her but was also leaving their little baby he knew nothing about, just eight weeks new growing inside her belly.

Beaufort, December 2019

"You and your mom say that to each other?" John asked Sayer, his brain not catching up with his words.

"Yeah, really cheesy, but it's something she has said to me my whole life. If I don't say it back, she repeats her part until I do," he laughed.

Silence.

"What is your mom's name?" he asked, holding his breath.

"Gaila. Gaila Penn," he stated, taking a bite of his warm barbecue sandwich. "Wow, this is actually really good!"

John could not stop staring at Sayer. He suddenly noticed that he had the exact same piercing blue eyes as Sayer, the same wavy, auburn hair.

"When's your birthday?" John asked.

"June 8," Sayer said, chomping away at his lunch. "1990."

"1990?" John asked.

"I know. I'm a millennial," Sayer said, rolling his eyes, knowing just how well John's generation despised his generation for their lack of work ethic.

John could not believe it. Gaila Penn. Could it be the same Gaila he loved many years ago? It had to be. This was not a coincidence.

"Are you okay?" Sayer asked.

John felt like his world was spinning. *I have a son. Has to be!*

"Ugh, yes, just a little tired," John lied, taking his first bite into his sandwich, still starting at Sayer.

"Oh, good, you look a little paler than you did a few minutes ago," he laughed. "Must be your old age."

"Hah," John started. "Must be."

As Sayer and John ate the rest of their lunches in silence, John couldn't help but think about Gaila. He wondered what she had been up to all these years, with a child, a boy, for that matter. It hadn't surprised him that she never reached out to him after leaving Salem all those years ago, but he needed to know why she felt like hiding the fact that they had a child together. *What caused her to do that?*

John thought back to his time with Gaila, their brief love story compared to their lifetime on earth. Although it was a short time, he had loved her thoroughly. Memories flooded his mind, including those of his own childhood. John recalled the very reason he left Salem in the first place.

As their lunch date ended, John and Sayer walked back to the old lobster boat. Sayer peered into the sky.

"It looks like those gray clouds are coming in fast," Sayer mentioned. "Maybe we should stop sooner today."

"Yeah, well, your generation doesn't like working through the tough times, do they?"

Sayer rolled his eyes, placing his phone on the captain's chair.

"I'm going down to check the rudder real quick. Where are the wet suits?" Sayer asked.

"Down in storage," John pointed.

"See you in a little bit," he said, taking off his shirt, exposing his tan skin.

John was not the one to snoop or invade another's privacy, but he had to get Gaila's phone number. Sayer finished getting on his wet suit and jumped in the water. John knew it was now or never. He walked over to his phone with his back to the end of the boat. He acted like he was playing with the controls.

*Recent Contacts:*

*Mom 12:30*

He flipped open his phone and quickly copied the number into his contacts, placing the phone down, his hands shaking.

John could not decide where and when, but he had to call Gaila to confirm his growing suspicion that he, in fact, had been united with their child. The child she had kept from him. And now their time together was almost over.

"I guess it's that time," Sayer said, putting his hand out to John.

"I guess so," John muttered, breaking eye contact with Sayer.

"Thank you, for everything," Sayer said. "You've taught me a whole lot more than just fixing up this boat."

"You know, I think I learned a thing or two from you too," John smiled.

"I think I owe you this," Sayer said, handing John a check.

"What's this?" John asked, glancing down.

"I'm buying the boat from you, like we promised."

"You seem to have forgotten the deal," John slyly remarked. "Take this boat where you want to go. I don't need the money. Just promise me you'll follow your heart this time."

"Are you kidding? I can't just take this boat."

"You can and you will," John insisted. "It's served its time with me, and now she's all yours," he said, handing Sayer the key.

"Are you sure? Is the motor still in there?" Sayer joked.

"Travel safe," John instructed. "If you ever need me, you know where I'll be."

"Thank you, for everything," Sayer said, bypassing John's hand and embracing him with a hug. John smiled, his cheeks on fire.

Sayer turned, and a fire lit up inside him. He knew what he needed to do. As he slowly turned on the motor and pulled out of the marina, he turned his boat north toward Marblehead. With a sigh and a smile, John too, knew where Sayer was headed.

Their time together had been worth it.

John grabbed his phone as Sayer and the pale blue lobster boat trailed off from view. He tapped on his screen, the light illuminating his blue eyes. His finger scrolled until he came upon Gaila's number. He punched her name, hearing the dial tone begin, his heartbeat thudding in his ears, his mind racing.

"Hello?" a soft, sweet voice answered.

John was still, his breathing shallow. It was her, after all these years. Before he could think to do anything else, he tore the phone away from his face and clicked *end call.*

# Chapter 14

New York, December 2017

I sla was busy at her office, noise from the honking of angry taxi's filling the room. Even behind the safety of a few doors and walls, she could not get away from this exuberant city.

"Ms. Wade?" Her secretary knocked on her door.

"Yes, come in Eliza!" she said, her eyes glued to her computer as her fingers noisily tapped on her keyboard.

"These came for you," she said, holding a large bouquet of red and orange calla lilies.

"What?" Isla said, staring at them.

"From a Mr. Walker," Eliza trailed.

"Um, yes, thank you," Isla said, getting out of her chair.

"They are beautiful," Eliza winked.

Isla blushed. "They are, aren't they?"

"Yes!"

Eliza turned to leave, not prying as much as she usually did. Isla sat, placing them to the right of her desktop computer. They were beautiful, their colors resembling her favorite season. She saw the card hidden within the bouquet.

*Dinner tonight? Please say yes—Fraunces Tavern @6:00pm*

*Yours, Walker*

Isla flashed a big smile. If this was how he treated her before committing to being boyfriend and girlfriend, she couldn't imagine what it was like being his.

She grabbed her phone, sliding up on the screen, clicking on her text message app. She knew he was probably anxiously awaiting her response.

Walker noticed his iPhone's screen light up. *It must be Isla,* he thought. Glancing down, he saw her name. *She must have just received them,* he thought. A sucker for cheesy romance, this will for sure lure her in. He looked across the table to his friend and brewery partner, Stan.

"One step closer," he mouthed.

"It worked?" Stan asked.

"Easy like Sunday morning," Walker laughed. Indeed, Walker set the hook, deeper than Isla would know for years to come.

"Welcome home!" Isla exclaimed. It was her and Walker's first week back to work since their honeymoon, and she wanted everything to be perfect.

"Hey," Walker sighed. He kicked off his shoes.

"Bad day?" Isla asked, frowning at the creases in his forehead.

"Why do you always assume it was bad?" he asked, his voice increasing with anger.

"I didn't. I just—" Isla tried to apologize. "I'm sorry."

"Well, you should be," he grumbled, walking past her.

"I made pasta!" she said, stirring the red meat sauce into the soft, al dente bow ties.

"I'm trying to stick to my Keto diet," he said. "I can't eat pasta."

"You didn't stick to Keto on our honeymoon," Isla retorted.

"Are you serious?" Walker yelled, his anger increasing by the second.

"Well, we ate and drank everything on the island; I thought you were done or something," she explained.

"So, you think I look like I ate and drank everything on the island?" he asked, slamming his hand down on the counter.

"Walker, no, stop being so sensitive," she said, noticing how much his patience had depleted.

"I'm not sensitive," he yelled, throwing the bowl of apples onto the ground, the glass shattering into a million tiny pieces on the floor. It had been a wedding gift from her father, handmade from Marblehead.

Isla stopped stirring the pasta, her heart racing.

"Walker, I'm sorry," she whispered, turning to face him.

"Sorry? Like that's just supposed to fix everything?" he screamed as he walked closer to Isla, his hand firmly grabbing her elbow. "Don't you ever put me down like that ever again, you hear me?"

Isla nodded, her body shivering.

"And if anyone doesn't need to be eating pasta around here, it's you," he hissed, whispering into her ear.

Walker let her go, her arm throbbing in pain. He walked past her and trudged up the loft to their room. Isla could not believe what he had just done. She grabbed her arm, noticing the bruise in the shape of his hand, making its mark on her body like a tattoo. She wiped her now flowing tears with her long-sleeve blouse, covering the now dark purple stain. She couldn't believe how sweet he was on their honeymoon, how gentle and tentative he was to her. Now, it seemed like he had thrown all of that out the window.

Aruba, Honeymoon

"Morning," Isla had whispered, kissing Walker's cheek as she slowly woke up. She could hear the waves breaking outside their window, the sunshine trying to peek its way into their room. Aruba was absolutely beautiful. It's blue skies never wavered, only raining late at night or early in the morning.

"Hmmm, good morning, my bride," Walker smiled, opening his eyes and returning a kiss to Isla.

"I love it when you call me that." She smiled.

"I love to call you that." He grinned.

"Room service?" she asked, slinking in behind him, curling her arms around his bare waist under the covers.

"Maybe in a little bit," Walker said, turning to face her. "Let's have some fun first." He pulled her toward him.

Later that day, after taking their places by the pool, they reclined peacefully in beach chairs, the sun kissing their bodies.

"Don't forget your sunscreen," Walker reminded her, tossing her the bottle.

"Thanks honey," she said, putting down her strawberry daiquiri.

As she lathered the sunscreen onto her body, she glanced at Walker.

"Babe?" Isla asked, noticing his attention on someone else.

Silence.

"Hello?" Isla said again, tossing the bottle of sunscreen at him to get his attention.

"Oh," Walker said quickly. "What's up?"

"Who are you looking at?" Isla asked, growing increasingly jealous.

"You, my queen," he assured her.

Isla rolled her eyes and let it go. She didn't want to be the one ruining their honeymoon over her new husband's wandering eyes at the pool. It was hard not to notice people in bathing suits. She glanced down at the two rolls on her stomach, a line forming in between them. She grew increasingly self-conscious.

"What do you want for lunch?" he asked, changing the subject.

"Sushi!" she smiled. "You?"

"That does sound good," he said. "Let me call our butler and order that really quick." He got up with the cell phone the resort had given them for the week. They could use it as often as they wished, asking their butler for whatever they fancied. He was to fulfill every wish with a reply of *yes, sir* or *yes, madam*. It made Isla feel awkward at first, but after the first two days, she felt like a celebrity. She decided to embrace it, and Walker didn't even seem fazed by it at all.

"Thank you," she said, taking another sip of her sweet frozen drink, closing her eyes to focus on the steel drums playing in the background.

Isla could not believe how relaxed she felt. After the first day, nothing could bother her. All the wedding drama had subsided, and they were what felt like a world away from their family members that had caused it. She felt like she could take a deep breath and exhale, with nothing stopping her.

"Another drink?" a waiter asked.

"Yes, please!"

"Another daiquiri?"

"That would be perfect," she said, handing the waiter her glass.

*I could get used to this*, she thought.

"Sushi is on its way," Walker smiled, laying back in his seat.

"Thank you, love," Isla gushed.

"You do look beautiful in that bikini," Walker gawked.

Isla knew she had to take her wardrobe up a notch on their honeymoon, so instead of the black one-piece bathing suit that she felt super comfortable in, she bought a tiny, black bikini trimmed with black lace. It screamed *"sexy,"* and her petite frame complimented it perfectly.

"Thank you," she laughed. "You are absolutely the sweetest."

"Anything for you," Walker said, reclining back in his chair.

In that moment, Isla felt she was where she was meant to be, with no care in the world, a certain wave of peace blanketing her, just as the warm sun.

Marblehead, July 2020

Isla sat out on the deck chair, fuming. How could her mother do this? Why would she tell him where she lived? It was like she was trying to ruin her life.

She picked up her phone.

"Oh, hello, darling," Patrice said, picking up the phone.

"Don't act like everything's okay," Isla started, her blood boiling.

"But everything is okay," she replied. Although Isla couldn't see it, she could hear how high her mother's nose had turned upward.

"Mom. I have had enough. First, you made Dad's funeral all about you and Grandma, and now you want to ruin what's left of my life!" she yelled.

"What on earth are you talking about?" her mother asked, the sarcasm flooding through the phone.

"You told Walker where I am, didn't you?" she hissed.

Pause.

"Well, you couldn't play house forever now, could you?" she retorted.

"You have no idea why I left New York. Why would you ever do that?" Isla scolded. "You have never cared about my life, not even enough to ask me about the most basic things."

"Because you can't have your cake and eat it too," Patrice said, clicking the phone shut.

"Hello . . . Mom?"

"What happened?" Sayer said, walking out to the deck to hand her a glass of water.

"I need something stronger than that," she grunted.

"Coming right up!" Sayer laughed, turning around.

Moments later, he came back out with a vodka tonic with three extra limes, just as she liked it.

"I'm guessing she acted like her normal self?" Sayer asked, sitting down across from her.

"At first, she tried to play dumb but then told me to stop playing house with you. She also told me that I can't have my cake and eat it too, whatever that means." Isla took a long sip of her cocktail.

"Sounds like her," he said, clinking his glass against hers. "Cheers to that." He laughed.

"Ugh." Isla sighed. "How am I going to fight this?"

"Do you want to fight him for it?" Sayer asked. "I'm sure you can find a lawyer."

Isla took a moment to answer, not sure how to articulate any words.

She took a deep breath. "I'm done with it. I'm so done with it," she confessed, feeling a weight lift from her shoulders. "It's nonstop working and phone calls. I never get a minute to myself. My staff is amazing, but I always doubt myself."

Sayer listened and watched Isla unload, something he grew fond of doing when they were younger. He noticed that she could always describe her feelings to him without hesitation. He loved how he made her feel that way, how she could feel so comfortable with him, still, after all this time. He loved watching her hands ricochet about, her eyes darting. He noticed the more annoyed she got, the faster she blinked. He understood her every move, anticipated it, even.

Sayer's eyes never left hers as she went on about her experience in New York. She didn't check her words as she spoke, didn't hesitate to be certain he wasn't getting angry or misunderstanding her. He nodded and held her hand tightly in his.

She could unload her thoughts on to him, and he bore the weight with her, never having to say a word back. He made her feel safe without trying.

"What do you think I should do?" she pleaded.

"I think you should write."

"What?" Isla whispered.

"Why don't you start a lit magazine in town, or even online? I'm sure there are other writers, even some young writers, who would contribute. You could do short stories and poetry. Think about you back then in high school, how much you loved writing poetry."

"I can finally live out my passion," she said, the light bulb clicking on in her brain.

"You can become a writer, here in Marblehead." He smiled.

Isla's eyes beamed at Sayer, her back straightening with excitement.

"People could also contribute art as well; it would be kind of a catch-all magazine for the arts!" she exclaimed, her eyes widening.

"Yes," he said. "Start off their dreams on the right foot."

"I love that!" she exclaimed.

"And I love you," Sayer smiled, squeezing her hand across the table.

Sayer was supportive, optimistic—the opposite of what Walker had been.

New York, December 2019

Walker had walked into their shared apartment, pristine in modern design. He found Isla on the island, her hands over her face, quietly crying to herself.

"Oh, honey," he said, dropping his things by the door, swiftly walking over to her, his arms extended. "What is it?"

Isla mumbled, muffled by sobs.

"What?" Walker asked, expecting something awful.

"They refused it," Isla whispered, wiping her eyes.

"Refused what? Who?" he asked, grabbing a napkin and offering it to her.

"The lit magazine, *Empire*, refused my poem." She buried her face in the napkin Walker had given her, her shoulders shaking.

Walker was surprised, not that she had been rejected, but by the fact that she had submitted a writing piece for publication. He couldn't recall any conversation about this.

Walker's brows knitted. "When did you submit it?"

"Six weeks ago," she shuddered. She dabbed her eyes to look up at him. "I let you read it."

"Is that a normal response time, six weeks?" he asked. He turned his face from hers to bite into an apple, not confirming that he remembered reading the piece.

"I guess so," Isla said, still dabbing at the unrelenting tears.

Long silent pause.

"Well, let's look on the bright side. You're still making money in real estate." He shrugged, wearing a smile as if nothing was wrong.

Isla stopped crying, her glassy eyes lifting to his.

"What?" she asked.

"I mean you still have a job, right?" He laughed.

"Well, I guess so, but I really love to write. This has been a dream of mine."

"Well, yeah, but a small dream," he mocked, walking over to the refrigerator, grabbing a cold craft beer.

"A small dream?" she said, not understanding his inability to empathize with her in that moment.

"I mean, come on, what's the percentage of people who actually get published their first go around?" he asked. "I mean, come on Isla, it's New York City for God's sake."

"I mean, I don't know," Isla said, her eyes dropping, her spirit crushed.

"I'm sure your poem was good, just not that good," he said, cracking open his beer, walking into the living room, flipping on the big screen TV.

Isla could not believe what she was hearing Walker say. He was nothing like the sweet, kind, empathetic man she had known up to this point. He used to be so attentive to her feelings in the beginning, but now, after a few months married, his true self had surfaced.

"Noted," she said, making a mental note never to share anything with him again. He cared more about money than her happiness.

"What?" he asked, not paying any more attention to their conversation.

"I'm going to take a bath," she said, running her fingers through her hair, walking up to their master bedroom.

"Want company?" he snickered.

"No," she stated.

When she got to the top of the stairs, she glanced down at him, wanting to see a reaction. But all she saw was him sipping his beer while watching the New York Giants football game, completely unfazed by her dig.

She undressed, catching a glimpse at herself in the bathroom mirror above the vanity. Her face resembled a raccoon, her eyes dark and red from her tears which wiped away her makeup, her elbow bruise from where Walker had grabbed her. She could see her ribs now, not wanting to gain any more weight for fear Walker would no longer be attracted to her. She stared at herself, a shell of a person, withering away like the dust from an old photograph. Her skin had become paler as the winter months set in, colorless, like her confidence toward herself.

As the warm water reached the top of the white porcelain tub, Isla turned the faucet off. Dipping her toes in first, she sank into the warm abyss, her stress melting away like butter. The cool eucalyptus bubbles floated along the length of her body, hugging her curves as she dipped under the water. Her world was quiet for a moment. Silence. Peace. When she emerged moments later, the bubbles came back, cradling her body once again like they never left. Another tear fell, and another behind that one. She felt lonely and unsatisfied. She was not who she used to be, and she was not who she wanted to become.

"There has to be more," she whispered to herself.

A few days later, it was Saturday night dinner with Walker's family.

"Hello, my handsome son," Mrs. Williams exclaimed, hugging Walker upon their arrival. "Isn't this place amazing?"

"One of my favorites!" Walker replied, giving his mother a light kiss on the cheek.

Isla stood off to the side, knowing she should follow his parent's lead. They weren't the biggest huggers with those outside their immediate family, even though she was considered one now.

"Hello, dear," Mrs. Williams said, acknowledging Isla's presence with a lithe smile.

"Lovely to be here," Isla responded, taking off her coat.

As they all took their seats, which Mrs. Williams had already planned out, Walker sat in between his parents while Isla took her seat opposite them, across the circular table.

"How is everything?" Mr. Williams asked Walker.

"Great, Dad. Time Hopp is booming, and business is on the rise. I think customers love the new brew, the coffee stout."

"Ah, yes. I'm so glad to hear," he said, patting his son's back. "It's also been a popular one back in Marblehead."

As his family continued to chat, Isla looked over the menu. She couldn't help but notice how they all probably wouldn't have minded if she were not there. They never asked her how the market was going or how many properties her company has recently sold. They just stayed consumed within each other. Deep down, she felt hurt, tormented by the fact that she had failed as a daughter in law. She didn't feel as if her own accomplishments mattered, her confidence obsolete.

"Isla, Walker tells us you've submitted some writing pieces to certain publications but were rejected. So sorry to hear that," Mr. Williams said.

"Oh," Isla gasped. "Yes, they didn't take my poetry."

"I'm sure something will happen for you," Mr. Williams said, turning to his son, suddenly changing the subject. "Besides, you have a business to run."

# Chapter 15

Marblehead High Junior Year, October 2007

The sweet scent of vanilla coffee being brewed had awaken Isla at an earlier hour than usual, before the sun fully peeked over the harbor. Her feet slid into her fuzzy slippers and draped her fleece, monogrammed robe over her shoulders. She took quiet steps down the stairs to find who else was awake.

"Mom?" Isla whispered.

"Well, good morning to you too," she smirked, taking a large sip of her coffee.

"You're never up this early." Isla grabbed a white coffee mug from the kitchen cabinet.

"Since when do you drink coffee?" Patrice asked.

Isla shot her mom a look. "I love coffee." She poured herself a hefty amount.

"There's cream in the fridge, if you like that," Patrice said.

"Thanks," she said, grabbing some from the fridge.

"I just couldn't sleep, a lot on my mind recently," she confessed, dropping into one of the chairs with a sigh.

Isla never had one-on-one talks with her mom; it was very rare for them to even converse for more than a few minutes with each other. And Isla's close relationship with her father clearly made her mother insecure. For whatever reason, Patrice hated the fact that her daughter and husband spent time together, although she would never show it. Patrice would make sarcastic remarks under her breath or criticize Isla outwardly in public. She loved nothing more than to embarrass Isla in front of her friends, secretly making up for her spoiled marriage. Isla could never understand why her mother was jealous. She figured it stemmed from her mother's shortcomings with her own father, something she never talked about.

Isla often wished their relationship was different. She would see how her other friends got along so well with their mothers and longed, for many years, to be just like them. Other mothers showed interest in their daughters, talked to them about school and relationships, made their daughters feel smart and empowered. Not Patrice. Whenever she could, she reminded Isla of all her failures, of never being good enough. Isla eventually internalized these moments, thinking it was something she was doing. Isla promised to do whatever it took to gain her mother's respect, no matter how cruel and twisted the circumstances seemed.

"Anything you want to talk about?" Isla asked.

"Not with you," she retorted.

Isla looked down at her coffee cup as hot steam swarmed her cheeks.

"Mom, I know we're not that close, but we can always change that," she mumbled, hoping for the best.

"Mothers and daughters are not supposed to be friends," she stated, getting up and walking out of the room.

Isla felt defeated. Every time she tried to make amends, she was reminded she was never up to her mother's standards. She vowed to herself, in that moment, that when she was older and if she ever had a daughter of her own, their relationship would be different. Isla felt deep in her heart that in a normal loving family, a child could have both—a parent and a best friend.

As a high school student, whenever Isla searched for clues for her mother's disdain, her mind drifted back to when she was a child. There was one scene in particular from the sixth grade that haunted her.

"Mom?" Patrice had asked while sitting quietly at the kitchen table.

"What is it?" her mother grumbled from the kitchen.

"Becky won't talk to me anymore," she said. "She chose to sit with the other girls at lunch and it really hurt my feelings."

"Well, what did you do to her?"

"What did *I* do?"

"Honey don't act stupid; it's not a good look. We all know your attitude. You must have done something to set her off."

"Well, I—" she started. "I don't remember having a disagreement with her about anything."

"Well then, I suggest you straighten out your personality before you try to make new friends. You're weak, Isla, and needy," she hissed, putting leftovers away in the refrigerator. "People admire strength."

Isla felt, deep down, that she could never be who her mother wanted her to be. She always assumed something was wrong with her. Weren't mothers supposed to take their daughter's side?

Isla's eyes slowly sputtered open after a long night's sleep, as if they were the wings of a new butterfly. Her arms stretched out and she could hear the light panging of pots and pans in the kitchen. As she sat up, she noticed Sayer's bike, resting on the side of the big oak tree just outside her window. She was still thinking about her encounter with her mother from the day before.

Sayer?

She jumped out of bed and ran her brush through her hair, making sure nothing was sticking up. She slipped her feet into her comfortable slippers. As she opened her bedroom door, she noticed a single Hershey kiss, then another and another making its way to the top of the stairs. A grin quickly appeared on Isla's face.

*What is he up to now?*

As she made her way down the steps, following the trail of Hershey kisses, she recognized the sweet aroma of pancake batter filling up the whole first floor of her family's home.

"Sayer?" Isla smiled, watching him flip pancakes in her kitchen. Isla's father sat at the table sipping his coffee with his eyes on the newspaper.

"Well, you didn't tell us you were dating a chef?" Ben smiled.

"Well, I didn't know!" she laughed.

"I'm making your favorite, blueberry pancakes," Sayer said, walking over to her and giving her a kiss on the cheek.

"Oh, my goodness, thank you," she gushed, hugging him back.

Isla's father was lovingly watching from the table, using the newspaper to block his smile.

"Where are we eating?" she asked, looking around and not seeing plates on the table.

"Outside!" Sayer smiled. "Look!"

Isla turned around to look outside through the big bay window in the kitchen. Although it was cold, Sayer had set up the table outside with heaters and blankets, and a fire was going in the fire pit.

"I thought it might be nice," he said. "If it's too cold, we can eat inside."

"It's perfect. Let me go put on a sweatshirt."

Isla ran up the stairs to her bedroom and grabbed her favorite old Boston University tattered maroon sweatshirt. She pulled it on over her head and quickly headed back downstairs. As she got to the kitchen, she noticed her mother had joined her father at the table. Isla was nervous about how her mother would react.

"Look what Sayer did, Mom!" she smiled, treading lightly.

"I can see," Patrice said. "That was very nice of him."

"Would you like some pancakes? I made plenty!" Sayer offered.

"Sure," Ben said.

"I'm alright," Patrice said.

"If you change your mind, I'll leave some here," Sayer said. "Come on, Isla!" He always knew how to cut the tension between Isla and her mother.

Isla grabbed her plate, noticing the heap of butter slowly melting down her warm pancakes, creating a pool of savory sweetness she could not wait to devour. Sayer opened the back door, where another trail of Hershey kisses led to their table. He had already poured orange juice in their cups and had a thermos filled with hot coffee. The warmth of the fire washed over them as they sat. Sayer gave her a blanket to put in her lap. As Isla looked out onto the ocean, she could see the sun slowly creeping above the horizon. Isla then realized she never looked at the time.

"Sayer, it's only seven! What time did you get here?"

"Six-fifteen," he said. "I went to the store yesterday to grab everything. I wanted to surprise you."

"Well, you did. It's amazing," she said, digging her fork into the pancakes.

They started to eat and chat about whatever came to mind. An easy, slow morning. The birds chirping in the distance created a serene peaceful feeling Isla could not describe. She wondered if their adult life together would be just as peaceful.

"I thought after we cleaned up, we could head into Boston, maybe walk around and window shop," Sayer said.

"I would really enjoy that." Isla smiled, placing her fork down on her plate.

"How were the pancakes? Edible?" he asked.

"Delicious!"

Marblehead, July 2020

With the divorce papers fresh on her mind, Isla went to bed late. She tossed and turned, unable to fully fall asleep. She must have, because when she woke up, she noticed the time on her iPhone.

Nine in the morning.

She turned on her belly and groaned into her pillow, stretching her arms and legs. As she did that, she didn't feel Sayer next to her.

"Sayer?" she called out.

"In here!" she heard him say from the kitchen.

She got out of bed, pulling on his oversized white T-shirt. She loved wearing his shirts; they looked like a dress on her petite frame. She could smell his old cologne still lingering on the collar. She pulled it to her nose, smiling.

*I've missed you*, she thought.

She opened the bedroom door and almost stepped on a trail of Hershey kisses making their way down the hallway. She followed them, smiling ear to ear. As she turned the corner, she saw Sayer slaving away in the kitchen, the record player on.

"Well, good morning!" he said, pulling her into him.

"Hi," she whispered, kissing his neck. "What are you doing?"

"Recreating our magic," he laughed, reaching over to the skillet where the blueberry pancakes were just about ready to be flipped.

"I love it," she smiled.

"Except, since we're adults now, we can have mimosas instead of just orange juice," he said, handing her a champagne glass.

"Yes!" she giggled, taking a long sip.

"I thought we'd eat outside. It's not too chilly out," he insisted.

"I am all in."

As they ate out on the back deck, admiring the ocean, Sayer smiled at Isla.

"We can do this every day, you know?"

"We can? What about work?" she winked.

"I mean we can be together every day if we want," he corrected.

"I would love nothing more," she smiled.

Sayer fumbled with his hands, not touching his food. Sweat appeared on his brow.

"You look like you're going to puke," she said, reaching for him.

Sayer got up from his chair to move closer to Isla. Her heart started to race, her adrenaline pumping.

"I've spent years wondering where you were and who you were with, kicking myself for ever letting you out of my life. Fate seems to have stepped in, and now I never want to be apart from you. Isla Wade, will you finally marry me?" Sayer stated, getting down on one knee, holding a beautiful princess cut diamond.

Isla gasped, a smile plastered on her face, tears starting to well up in her eyes.

"I never want to be anywhere else . . . YES!" she gushed, hugging him first and totally bypassing the ring.

They kissed, Sayer gently placing his hand under her jaw line, his other hand on her lower back.

"I knew, deep down, we were going to come back to each other." She smiled, resting her forehead onto his.

"I felt it too, when I first noticed you again at *Tina's* my first afternoon back in Marblehead," he said.

They kissed again, both of their worlds complete.

"I guess you should wear this now!" Sayer laughed, finally placing the ring on her left hand, where it should have lived many years ago.

That afternoon, they made love, entangled, dreaming up the life they had always wanted to live, finally with each other. Later that night, while eating dinner inside by candlelight, Sayer knew they needed to address the elephant in the room.

"Where are you with those divorce papers? Did you mail them back?"

Isla paused, already knowing this had been weighing on his mind.

"I met with my dad's lawyer a few days ago, in town," she explained. "I decided to give him everything."

"Everything? Like your family's company?" Sayer choked on his dinner.

"Yes," she said confidently. "It doesn't fit inside the life I want to create with you."

"How do you know you're making the right decision?" he asked.

"My dad," she smiled. "Here, I'll show you."

She got up to get her father's letter, still hiding in her purse. After handing it to Sayer, she could see how meticulous he was reading it. With so much care and attention. When he finished, he looked up at her.

"Well, that helps."

"Unexpectedly," Isla added.

"Are you sure, Isla? We can live in New York if you want. I have no preference," Sayer said.

"I appreciate that, but we both will be happiest here in Marblehead," she said, holding up her glass for him to clink.

A few days later, Isla met her dad's lawyer and friend.

"Hello, Isla," Mr. Schmidt said, engulfing her in a bear hug.

"Hello, Mr. Schmidt!" She wrapped her arms around him.

"I wish we could meet under different circumstances," he started.

"I know," Isla sighed.

"So, your mother moved power of attorney to you; you already stated you were all right with that," he explained. "Your mother said that she could not bear anymore hardship with making decisions with your father's things."

"Yeah, I got that line too," Isla sighed. "However, I'm not sure if you do this kind of thing, but can I ask for your professional opinion?"

Isla grew up knowing how close her dad was to his lawyer friend. Mr. Schmidt was often at their house, sharing a bourbon outside with Ben or having a business meeting in his office at home. He was a simple man, generous to everybody. Ben trusted Mr. Schmidt with is life.

"Of course you can," Mr. Schmidt smiled.

"I have recently moved my whole life in New York City to be back here in Marblehead, only, I'm leaving one thing behind," she paused. "Walker."

"I see," Mr. Schmidt stated as Isla handed him the divorce papers.

"Walker sent me these, and his intentions are pretty clear." She pointed to the part where he wished to have complete authority over her family's real estate business.

Mr. Schmidt's eyes grew larger.

"I know," Isla sighed again. "It's a huge deal."

"It is," he said. "What was your first reaction upon opening this?"

"I was angry, but I know I've given up so much of myself in New York. It was beautiful, and I worked like a dog, but I'm just not sure I want to continue that lifestyle. My heart isn't in it."

"Well, before you showed me this, I had something your father wanted me to give you, upon his last request," Mr. Schmidt said, putting the papers down.

"What?" Isla asked, dumbfounded.

"A few weeks before your father's passing, we had our bi-annual meeting where we review his will and go over finances," he explained. "He came here with this." Mr. Schmidt fumbled through some papers, then a letter emerged in his hands. "He explained that if anything ever happened to him, he wanted you to have this."

Isla was stunned, her eyes transfixed on the letter in Mr. Schmidt's hands. She could not bring herself to look at him. Her hands began to shake.

"I never got to say goodbye," she confessed.

"Think of this as his goodbye," he kindly said, placing the letter in front of her, "I will leave this here and step out. You can review it, and we can talk about your divorce afterwards. It might be of help to you."

Mr. Schmidt placed the letter in front of her, got up, and closed the door behind him. Her ears began to ring, and her heart began to race.

*To my beautiful daughter, Isla*

She turned the envelope over, her mind trying to imagine her father writing this letter. This letter contained their last conversation, everlasting words that she could read on forever. Maybe that's why he wrote another letter, per their ritual. It was another shift in her life, her childhood into adulthood. Although he wasn't physically there, he wanted to give his advice one last time. Isla's lips quivered as she opened the back of the letter, stopping when she spotted his handwriting. Letters were so intimate, his words carefully crafted. She felt honored he chose her. She stopped, looking around Mr. Schmidt's office to make sure she was alone. As her hands trembled, she unraveled the fragile letter.

*My dearest Isla,*

*If you are reading this, I am no longer Earth-side. I'm not sure how my life will end, but I just wanted to be prepared to say goodbye in case I couldn't say this in person. You are the absolute light of my life. When your mother and I found out we were having a girl, I could not contain my excitement. I knew you would be strong-willed, feisty, and a force to be reckoned with. You have done everything right. You have exceeded all my expectations, even your mother's, of which she will probably never admit to you. Ultimately, you do not need our blessings in any endeavors you may choose for your life, but you do have mine.*

*I want you to live your life on your own terms. I want you to chase any goals you wish to run after. Do not, and I mean this, do not stay in real estate if it does not excite you. It does not matter in the long run; it is what makes you happy that does. I want you to turn whatever pain you are feeling into passion. Travel wherever you wish to go. You only get this life once.*

    *I have loved you for what seems my entire life, my sweet daughter.*

    *Go give 'em hell!*

*Love,*
*Dad*

Isla's eyes watered, and tears streamed. She could not believe what she had just read. Her father, once again, helping her through to her next chapter, even after departing this life.

"Mr. Schmidt?" Isla called. "I know what I need to do."

# Chapter 16

As the days before her wedding to Sayer approached, Isla couldn't help but to think about the disappointment of her wedding to Walker some five years earlier. Her new life with this wonderful man from her past, would be better, a fresh start. The past was the past, but it still lingered. Only the future would bury it. Still the memory of her wedding day to Walker stung.

Marblehead, October 2015

"Girl, wake up. You're getting married today!" Kelly had exclaimed, busting into Isla's bridal suite.

"What the—" Isla shouted, just waking up.

"You ready?" Kelly yelled again, this time jumping on her bed.

"I guess so," Isla yawned, rubbing her eyes. "What's the weather like?"

"Well," Kelly paused. "Right now, it's a little cloudy, but it's supposed to brighten up later."

"I hope so," Isla said, sitting up.

"Here." Kelly handed her a champagne glass. "Drink this mimosa so you won't worry about the weather all morning."

"All right!" Isla smiled. "Let's get this day started."

Kelly and Isla waited in their bathrobes, cuddled up in bed, for the hair and makeup team who were set to arrive shortly.

"You ready?" Kelly asked, taking another swig of her drink.

"Yeah," Isla shrugged.

Kelly put down her drink. "Well, that screams excitement."

"There's so much that's about to happen. This, right now, is quite literally the calm before the storm. I'm trying to stay calm."

"But you're excited, right?" Kelly asked again.

"Yeah," Isla nodded with more confidence. "I just hope everything goes as planned."

Isla was a closet perfectionist on certain things. Her room? No. Her car? Not a chance. But her wedding? Yeah, it was going to be perfect whether she killed herself making it possible or not.

"Well, I just want you to sit back and enjoy it. I feel like it's going to go by really fast," Kelly explained.

"I will," Isla promised.

*Knock, knock.*

"They're here!" Isla perked up.

Isla got off the bed to open the door to greet the hair and makeup team, ignoring her friend's watchful eye.

After two hours, both girls were ready to put their dresses on. Isla's wedding gown was hanging from the ceiling, draped over the sliding door to the balcony. Although the sun wasn't completely shining, the dress's subtle crystals lit up the room.

"It's so beautiful," Kelly said. "It looks different than when you tried it on in the shop."

"Yes," Isla placed her fingers across the soft white lace. "I added the scalloped bottom and made the train longer. Walker's mother insisted."

"I love it," Kelly said. "I just would have thought you would pick something simpler."

"I know. I thought that too," Isla said. "But when am I ever going to do this again? Might as well go big, right?"

"I guess," Kelly said. "Were those alterations expensive?"

"Walker's mom offered to pay for it. She loved the idea of adding more," Isla explained.

"*Hmm,*" Kelly mumbled, tracing her finger over the trim with a frown.

The rain had begun. At first it was a slight drizzle, but then it turned into an all-out storm. Isla stared out the window, standing there in her dress, one hand by her side, the other holding the curtain open. The gray clouds engulfed the sky and her mood changed. She could see the workers at the Penn's Brewery stumbling around, grabbing and wiping down all the wet chairs that had been set out in preparation the night before. She felt, deep in her soul, this wasn't supposed to be happening; it wasn't what she had envisioned her wedding day to be. Her heart dropped, a deep aching pulling at her stomach. She hadn't eaten a full meal in days, trying to prepare to fit into her dress. Her future mother-in-law reminded her to fast to keep the bloat away.

"Dear?" Ben said, slowly walking through the door to where Isla was standing.

Isla's eyes didn't leave the window.

"This is terrible," she cried, finally turning around.

"Your wedding planner has been running around. She says we can fit everything in the barn. That might be the best they can do," he said.

"Everyone's going to hate it," Isla frowned, her father walking closer to her.

"It doesn't matter, honey," Ben said, grabbing his daughter's hands. "You look beautiful and that's all Walker's going to care about."

"Is Mrs. Williams furious?" Isla asked, knowing that her mother-in-law must be ordering everybody around.

"I'm not sure who is angrier, your mother or Mrs. Williams." He laughed.

"I bet it's a real shit-show." Isla smiled.

"There it is," Ben said, lightening the mood. "I love it when you smile."

"I just want everything to be perfect," she said, letting her shoulders sink down after being tense all morning.

"It will be," he promised. "Because you are the bride today."

Isla smiled, looking up at her father. "Now, let's go give 'em hell!" he exclaimed.

As Isla stood inside the barn, her guests patiently waiting for her to start her descent down the long aisle, she saw her mother and Mrs. Williams scowling at each other from their respective sides. The flowers hadn't been able to be saved due to all the rain and wind, but what they could save was safely set on the alter, where her and Walker would be saying their vows. The string lights were above everybody's heads, twinkling just like they were supposed to.

*A silver lining,* Isla thought.

The violin quartet started up, and her nerves ran ramped.

"You ready?" Ben asked, leaning down toward Isla.

"I think so," she whispered.

"Because if you're not, we can go. I can tell everybody to go home."

"Dad," she rolled her eyes.

Mr. Wade tightened his grip on Isla's arm, wrapped around his. The doors opened and everyone turned to face them, smiles darting across their faces. She could feel her long trail tugging gently on the floor, her feet moving slowly, one foot in front of the other. She felt awkward, like everybody was waiting for her to trip, mess up, or run.

"Deep breaths," her father whispered.

Isla smiled up at him, always trying to calm her down, even as a grown woman on her wedding day. People were taking pictures with their cell phones, after being told no flash photography, and that made Isla tense. She didn't like giving up control like that, not being able to see what they were posting or being able to see how she looked. Her jaw tightened as she looked up to Walker. He was smiling. Beaming, actually. She hoped that he would cry, show some emotion, but he didn't.

*Another let down.*

Ben stopped at the altar, giving Isla a soft kiss on the cheek. Walker took Isla's hand and the service started. Within fifteen minutes, they were married. All of that hype for what seemed like a minute, her world moving slower as Kelly handed her back her bouquet of white and pink roses. She looked down at them, a pang of anger running through her veins. Her mother had switched out the bouquet last minute; she had felt lilies were "only for funerals." How did she not notice before walking down the aisle?

She looked up at her mother while everyone clapped and cheered, her mother standing still, a pained expression on her face.

Her wedding day was not what she had imagined, not even a little bit. She looked up at her new husband, Walker, who was waving and cheering at everyone else, not even glancing at his new bride or telling her how beautiful she had looked.

Had she just made the biggest mistake of her life?

Isla awoke from her and Sayer's fluffy white bed as a good morning kiss softly landed on her cheek.

"Good morning, love," Sayer whispered. "Let's get married today."

"Is that today?" Isla laughed, rolling around and kissing him on the tip of his nose.

"Very funny," he smiled, pulling the comforter over their heads, tickling her sides.

"Oh my goodness," she squealed.

They both started laughing, stopping to kiss one another. Sayer put one hand behind her head and the other around her chin, kissing her so passionately. Isla stopped squirming, giving in to his embrace.

Sayer pulled away. "Let's get ready," he whispered.

"I'm going to shower," Isla said, kicking off the covers.

"Sounds good," Sayer smiled, watching her leave. "You look beautiful."

"Thanks, honey," she smiled.

Isla walked into the bathroom, slowly turning on the shower to get the right temperature. The clean white marble looked so bright in the mornings, the gold mirror illuminating the soft features on her makeup-less face. She glanced at herself, a whole new sense of confidence. Over the last few months, she learned to love the natural curl to her hair, the slow fade of her highlights. Her skin was smooth without makeup, but she didn't appreciate it until now. Sayer had a lot to do with all of that. Always complimenting her on her natural self, helped her reveal to herself the power within. She never relied on her own happiness because of him; he just knew how to encourage her. It was with his encouragement that she felt comfortable in her own skin. The rolls on her tummy no longer bringing about self-hatred. The cellulite on her thighs was okay, because that meant she was healthy enough to live another day. All the things that she felt like she needed to hide in the past were assets in her life now. She could not be more thankful.

As Isla got into the shower and lathered her body in shea butter body wash, she heard the shower door creek open.

"Here you go," Sayer smiled, handing her a champagne glass.

"In the shower?" she laughed.

"Why not?" he chuckled, jumping in with her.

"Cheers, to many more weekends like this," Sayer said, clinking his glass with hers.

"Cheers!" she giggled, taking a sip and letting him kiss her again, this time for longer.

After their shower, Sayer made blueberry pancakes, Isla's favorite.

"I think we need to be at the overlook at noon," Sayer said, reminding Isla of the plan.

"Sounds good," Isla said. "Your mom knows, right?"

He flipped the last pancake from the pan. "Yes. Did you remind Kelly?"

"She is all set. She should be here soon." Isla glanced at the clock.

"Perfect," he said, handing her a plate with a fork and knife.

Kelly arrived shortly after, beaming with excitement.

"Are you ready for today, you two?"

"Yes," they both said, smiling ear to ear at each other.

"Well, good, it sounds like it should be all sun for today." She winked at Isla.

"And even if it rains, I wouldn't mind one bit," Isla stated, her eyes twinkling.

"That's what I like to hear!" Kelly said, pouring herself a large glass of champagne. "Okay, eat those pancakes, and we are going to get ready," Kelly instructed.

Once breakfast was all cleaned up, Kelly dragged Isla into their bedroom where Isla's wedding dress hung on display from the back of her closet door.

"It's stunning," Kelly gushed.

"I love it too," Isla smiled, staring at the simple, short lace shift dress she had chosen.

"This is more you," Kelly said, walking over to it, her fingers softly running along the delicate lace.

"Agreed."

"So, for your hair," Kelly clasped her hands. "I'm thinking half up with flowy curls. Thoughts?"

"I like that!" Isla said, sitting on her chair in front of her small vanity.

"Of course, we'll go light on the makeup. I think Sayer likes that more." Kelly smiled, hugging Isla who was sitting in front of her mirror. "I'm so happy for you. I must say."

"I am too. Thank you for being here," Isla said, already starting to tear up.

"We can't cry, not now!" Kelly shouted, wiping away the clouds in her eyes.

It was finally noon as Sayer, Isla, and Kelly pulled up to their favorite overlook in Marblehead, right across from Old Burial Hill.

"I see the officiant's car!" Kelly announced. "That's a good sign."

"Yeah, tell me about it." Sayer laughed.

"Mr. Schmidt's never late to anything," Isla said.

As the three of them trudged up the old concrete stairway to the top of the lookout, Isla spotted an extra car hugging the edge of the road. It was only supposed to be the five of them, Isla and Sayer, Kelly and Gaila, and of course the officiant. Who could be driving that Camry?

When they got to the top, the view stole all their attention—the dark navy ocean, the crisp orange and yellow leaves stealing the show.

"It's beautiful." Gaila smiled, walking over to Isla, giving her a hug and kiss on the cheek.

"It's perfect," Isla said in return, embracing Gaila.

"Let's get you two married." Mr. Schmidt smiled.

Everyone took their place. Isla and Sayer faced with their hands joined, while Kelly and Gaila beamed by their sides.

As Mr. Schmidt cleared his throat, another person emerged from the stairwell.

"I hope I'm not too late," John muttered.

Gaila froze as she turned around, staring straight into John's eyes. Her mouth fell open.

"John?" Gaila whispered.

"John, you made it!" Sayer smiled. "But how—" He started, now noticing his mother's still expression.

"Gaila," John said, slowly walking forward, still a few feet away.

"How?" Gaila muttered, not sure how to react.

"Mom, you know him?" Sayer asked.

"Well, yes," Gaila responded. Her mind hadn't caught up with her eyes. Her hands shook, and she tried to steady them against her stomach.

"I know it's been a long time," John started, staring at her. The wind caught the corner of his suit and tussled it, but he remained steady in his stance. "I became good friends with your son before I realized who he was."

"Wait, I'm confused," Sayer said. Isla watched all of this unfold, her hand cupped firmly over her mouth.

"Sayer, this is your father, John," she smiled.

"My father?" Sayer asked, flabbergasted. His hands dropped to his sides.

"Yes," Gaila said. A tear rolled down her cheek.

"I didn't know that when we were in Beaufort," John said to Sayer. "I promise you that."

Gaila took a tender step forward. "You two were together?" She asked, astonished.

Sayer glanced between the two of them. "Well, yes. We worked on the lobster boat together in Beaufort," he explained. "But I had no idea he was my father. I should be asking you that, mom!"

"We dated, many years ago," she explained.

"Mom?!" Sayer asked. His knees wobbled, and he reached for Isla to steady him. She held tight. "Why didn't you—?" He couldn't find the words. Tears glazed over his eyes.

"Don't blame her," John interjected. "I left without knowing about you."

Gaila's voice cracked as she spoke. "You had so much going on in your life John, I didn't want to overwhelm you. I wanted you to follow your dreams, not resent me, or our son, for the rest of your life," She took a tender step toward him.

"I could never have resented you, Gaila," John said, holding her hands in his. "And I'm so proud of you for raising such an amazing young man on your own."

Isla gasped.

"You were on the plane with me," she uttered. "The night I left New York City."

John stared into her eyes, a big smile erupting. "That was a pleasant coincidence that I got to meet you."

"You talked me through the flight. I remember you," Isla said, "but why were you in New York?"

"Visiting my sons. They live in Manhattan," he explained.

"Sons?" Gaila smiled.

"Yes, two of them," John laughed.

Kelly just stood there, slack-jawed by all that was unfolding.

"I can't even fathom this," Sayer said excitedly, walking over to John and extending his arms for a hug.

"I'm sorry I didn't tell you sooner, Sayer. But I only learned as you were leaving Beaufort, and I wasn't certain yet to say anything," he explained. "But then I got your invite."

"I don't blame you," Sayer said, holding his father in a long hug. "I'm just so glad you're here. You've changed me and made me realize all of this." He held his hands out over the ceremony. "I couldn't imagine you not here. Thank you for figuring out you were my dad, when I was too blind to see it."

John wiped a tear from his own eyes. "I heard you on the phone with your mother one afternoon, and when you hung up with her, I couldn't believe what I was hearing." He smiled at Gaila. "She and I used to end our calls with that same line."

"Until the end," Gaila started.

"Forever and always," John finished. "I still remember."

Gaila smiled right back, tears welling up in her eyes.

"I even tried to call you," John started to explain, "but once I heard your voice. I hung up."

"Don't cry, Mom," Sayer said, holding his arm out, touching his mother's shoulder.

"They're happy tears," she said, wiping them off her cheek.

"Well, they better be. We have a wedding today!" Mr. Schmidt belly laughed.

"Oh, that's right," Gaila said. "John, would you like to watch our son get married?"

"I would love to." He beamed, taking his place next to Gaila.

"All right," Mr. Schmidt said. "Where were we?"

Within ten minutes, Isla and Sayer were married, their happiness restored. As they kissed each other, solidifying their marriage, they both smiled at each other, tears overwhelming their eyes.

Finally, their long journey concluded.

"I'm yours," Isla sweetly whispered, her lips flirting with Sayer's ear, "unapologetically."